THE SPRING BRIDE

CLAIRE SANDERS

For Giuliana: I look forward to seeing what you will do with your bright future.

CHAPTER ONE

The town of Brightfield differed little from every other farming community in the state. Family farms surrounded the town center where the grocer, the butcher, and the pharmacist opened their shops at ten and closed promptly at six. Friendly competition among the townspeople kept the lawns meticulously mowed, seasonal flowers in gardens, and houses freshly painted. On Sundays and national holidays, most homes flew the country's new flag with stars for all forty-six states.

The one exception to the town's beauty was a smattering of ten shacks located behind the freight depot at the edge of town. Originally built for railroad workers, they now served to house the families of men who drifted from place to place searching for work. Each successive owner had neglected the property until the small homes resembled the toothless smiles of mummified skulls.

George Mason, however, did not think the shacks were a disgrace. As he stood in the courtyard of the small community, he smiled. The new owner had hired him to demolish the dilapidated houses and build new homes, making it possible for George to finally move from handyman to business owner. Mason Construction Company would have a business office and employees. If his dreams came true, he would one day be the head of the largest construction firm in the state. In fifty years, when people spoke about the history of his company, they would say it all started in Brightfield, way back in 1911, with ten shacks behind the freight depot.

A whisper of a spring breeze ruffled his hair, a sign winter would soon end. The neighborhood was oddly quiet for a Monday morning. The older children were undoubtedly in school, and the men were probably working, but where were the wives and babies? The fluttering of a curtain caught his attention. A toddler's dirty face peeked through the window followed by the unmistakable wail of an unhappy baby. George couldn't blame the residents for keeping to themselves. Their homes had recently been transferred to a new landlord, and now a strange man stood in the dusty courtyard. Change was in the air.

A familiar red and white Oldsmobile rolled to a stop on the gravel road leading to the houses. His new sister-in-law got out of the automobile and lifted a hand in greeting. Hildy Campbell had been a welcome addition to the Mason family, although his brother's wedding had caught George by surprise. He'd never suspected Andrew had the nerve to court the most successful businesswoman in town.

"Good morning, George." Hildy said as she approached.

"Mornin'." He gestured toward the folder she had tucked under one arm. "Are those the plans you've decided on?"

"Yes. These are summary drawings for five different houses. The actual blueprints are at my house. I thought you could build two of each, but paint them differently, and don't place the duplicates too close to each other. I also bought the adjacent lots, so you'll have plenty of space. I never realized how high the demand for low-cost rental housing is, so I want to get started as soon as possible."

"No problem there. Work should go fast now that the worst of the winter weather is over. Did you include the survey as well?"

"Yes." Hildy passed the folder to George. "There's also a check for you. It should be enough to buy the materials and hire workers. When you need more, let me know."

A morsel of apprehension landed in his stomach. He wasn't known for saying the right thing at the right time, but he needed to thank Hildy for making his dream come true. "I hope you know how much I appreciate —"

Hildy waved away his gratitude. "George, I know we're family now, but this is a business deal, pure and simple. You're going to demolish these shacks and build houses I intend to rent. We'll both make money."

The people who lived in the shacks paid a mere pittance for rent. Hildy intended to improve their lives by building modest, comfortable homes without raising the amount they paid. No wonder his brother had fallen in love with her. She wouldn't make a profit from the houses for many years, but she realized replacing the dilapidated houses would benefit the whole community. Children would be healthier, residents could have low-cost housing without sacrificing their dignity, and the town of Brightfield would no longer be ashamed of the blighted neighborhood.

Hildy turned slowly to take in the entire site. "I can't wait to walk through the first home."

George tucked the folder under his arm. "I'll do the best I can."

Hildy's broad smile relaxed George. "I already knew that. Now, I'm on my way to Greenville for a board meeting of Superior Farm Machinery."

"And I'm going to the bank to open an account for my new business."

Hildy squeezed George's arm in a gesture of affection. "I'll see you Sunday if not before."

George lifted his hand in farewell. "Tell my little brother to behave himself." He watched Hildy expertly turn her car around and drive away. He couldn't wait to buy his first automobile, although a dray should probably come first. He'd need a heavy wagon for transporting building supplies.

He opened the folder and removed the check. One glance and goosebumps rose on his skin. Twenty thousand dollars? George had never seen so much money in one place. How rich was Hildy? It was widely known her father had left her well-off, but George had never imagined she could casually write such a large check.

With this windfall, he could buy a truck. They were advertised as capable of carrying a half-ton load, something he'd never accomplish efficiently with horses and wagons. With twenty thousand dollars he could purchase all the building materials, rent a warehouse for storage, and hire enough men to finish the houses quickly.

A hundred tasks lay ahead of him, but his excitement couldn't be subdued. He'd make a list and accomplish each one step-by-step. Right after he opened that bank account and deposited the biggest check he'd ever seen, he'd force himself to sit and plan.

***

In the Brightfield Medical Clinic, Greta Franklin filed the last chart, closed the account book, and cleared her desk of the day's work. It was her favorite time of day. Dr. Connor saw patients in the clinic from eight o'clock till noon, had lunch with his wife, and then made house calls. When he left the office, Greta could take charge. A sense of well-being enveloped her whenever she put everything to right — the charts in alphabetical order, the examination room spic and span, and the papers on Dr. Connor's desk categorized in order of importance. In the clinic, she was needed and appreciated. If only the rest of her day brought similar feelings.

After her busy mornings, she walked to the clean but simple room she rented in Brightfield's only boarding house. There she waged a daily battle against loneliness and despair. On Wednesdays, she subdued her emotional enemies by participating in the Ladies' Circle at her church. On Fridays, she searched the library for books she hadn't read. And on Sundays…

Sundays were the hardest days of all. She rose early for church and faithfully volunteered with the children's Sunday School. Then she sat in the back of the sanctuary for Sunday services. But after church, she had to face her weekly letdown. After a morning filled with friendly people and the heartwarming message from the minister, she returned to an empty room where the hours crept by with painful apathy.

Those were the hours when she missed her parents the most. She wrote them letters about her happy new life in Brightfield, the wonderful young doctor for whom she worked, and the friends she'd made at church, but she never mentioned her husband. That was her private shame. No one knew the truth except Dr. Connor, and he'd taken an oath to protect her secret.

As Greta locked the clinic door and set out toward the boarding house, she wondered how she would fill that afternoon. Based on the librarian's recommendation, she'd borrowed a new book titled *Howard's End*. The title puzzled Greta, but perhaps she'd start the novel this afternoon. She had nothing else to do.

***

On Wednesday afternoon, George cleared his mother's kitchen table and rolled out the first set of blueprints. Hildy had chosen the new Craftsmen bungalows being marketed by Gustav Stickley, a choice George heartily endorsed. There was something uniquely American about the small, efficient houses. They lacked pretension and ornamentation but featured practical additions like built-in bookcases and wide fireplace mantels. The Craftsmen house didn't have the ornamentation of the older Victorian residences in town. It was as if there was no need to shout when honesty and confidence would win the day.

He used empty cups to weigh the edges of the plans while he compared the house's foundation to the land survey. Hildy wanted indoor plumbing and heat in each house, so George would have to tap into the city's water and gas systems. All of which meant underground pipes. The first stop would be town hall to find out how the utilities could be managed. Only the poorest people still used kerosene lanterns to light their houses, so the electric company would also need to be consulted.

He turned to a clean page in the cloth-bound blue notebook he used. So much to do. He didn't want Hildy to know he'd never built a house before, and to George's way of thinking, the best way to learn was by doing. But the list of things to buy and people to see was growing longer. What he really needed was someone who could guide him along the way.

The kitchen door opened, letting in a warm breeze that ruffled the edges of the blueprints. His father and older brother entered, their heavy footsteps tracking in mud from the fields.

"Out!" his mother shouted, pointing to their boots. "You know better than to dirty my floor!"

Where had his mother come from? George had been in the kitchen alone, but one muddy boot had caused her to materialize like magic.

John dropped immediately and unlaced his boots. His father, however, held out his arms. "Oh sweetheart," he said with a grin. "Come and give me a kiss."

His mother crossed her arms over her chest and glared at his father. "I'll give you a kiss when you've cleaned the mess you've made."

His father put a hand over his heart. "How you wound me " He braced himself by putting a hand on John's shoulder and toed off his boots.

John took the boots to the porch. "I'll clean the floor," he volunteered. "The last thing I want is Mom angry with me."

Wearing only his socks, George's father silently crossed the kitchen and wrapped his arms around his mother. "Am I forgiven?" He kissed her cheek. "Are you too angry to make us some coffee?"

"Go on with you," his mother said with a laugh. "Coffee's on the stove. I'm off to the Ladies Circle."

His father kissed her again before releasing her. Then he retrieved three cups and filled them with hot coffee.

George smiled at the scene. His parents were often affectionate with each other, their enduring love an example of what George someday wanted for himself. But so far, Cupid hadn't found the right woman for him. Many ladies were cowed by his size, but George couldn't simply change his body. At six feet six inches he towered over everyone in Brightfield, and his brawny physique had developed through the years of farm work. In school, he'd been called Hercules and Goliath, nicknames he didn't like but had learned to laugh about.

"I'll be home around five o'clock," his mother called as she gathered her hat, gloves, and handbag. "George, I still need you to check the shutters."

Guilt nipped at George's conscience. He'd forgotten the shutters. Better do it soon because once he started on Hildy's houses, there would be no time for handyman jobs. "I'll take care of it today, Mom."

John opened the door for her. "I'll hitch the buggy for you."

She smiled at her sons. "Thank you, boys. There's chocolate cake for dinner tonight."

George watched his mother as she and John walked through the door. Chocolate cake was just one of the ways his mother rewarded her sons. He would have helped his mother without the rewards, but he'd never been known to turn down a slice of cake.

His father set a cup of coffee in front of George and sat in a straight-backed chair across from him. "Blueprints? I've never seen you with anything like that before."

George sipped the black coffee. "I wouldn't want Hildy to know, but this is the first time I've seen blueprints. I may be in over my head, Dad."

His father studied him across the table. "What do you mean?"

"Hildy doesn't want a simple repair. She expects me to build ten houses with indoor plumbing, gas lines for cooking and heating, and electricity. Maybe I should have admitted I don't know how to do all that."

"Why didn't you?"

"I've always learned by doing. I didn't know how to repair the plumbing in Benjamin's clinic until I actually had to do it."

"You figured it out."

"Yep. But this…" He gestured to the building plans. "This is more complicated."

"Do you have a deadline?"

"Not exactly, but Hildy's put twenty thousand dollars into this venture, and she's going to expect results."

His father drank his coffee in silence for several minutes before replying. "I think my new daughter-in-law is a reasonable person. Why not tell her you need to hire help?"

"I've got the funds to hire workers, but who should I hire to teach me? So far, I've paid by the job — Joe Thompson for painting, Adam Mack for bricklaying — but I don't know anyone who can advise me about this."

His father got to his feet and circled the table so he could look over the blueprints. He rubbed his chin as he flipped through the pages. "I'm like you, son. I know a good bit of carpentry, but I've never built from blueprints. Have you considered Henry Mitchell?"

George frowned at his father. "Isn't he too old?"

"I imagine his days of climbing ladders and lifting heavy loads are over, but his brain still works just fine. Henry was a construction supervisor in Greenville. Worked on houses and commercial buildings."

George had met Henry Mitchell but didn't know him well. "How old is he?"

His father stuck out his bottom lip as he thought. "Don't rightly know. Older than I am but not by much."

"Think he'd be interested?"

"There's only one way to find out. Why don't we ride over there?"

"John doesn't need you?"

"Nah. Ground's too wet for tilling, so he's checking fences today."

George rolled the blueprints and returned them to the cardboard tube they'd come in. "I'm ready when you are. Want me to hitch the wagon?"

"John's using it. Let's saddle the last two horses."

George stood, tucked the blueprints under his arm, and opened the door for his father. "Hope Henry doesn't mind us dropping in."

His father walked through the door and sat on the top step of the back porch to put on his boots. "If he greets us with a shotgun, we'll simply turn around."

George didn't know Henry Mitchell very well, but the twinkle in his father's eye meant he'd been joking about a gun. "As long as I can run faster than you, there's no need for me to worry."

His father hooted a laugh and reached for his other boot. George ambled toward the barn, the sound of his father's laughter following him like the dancing tail of a kite.

***

Greta had just finished organizing Dr. Connor's desk when she heard footsteps in the hall. The familiar face of Abigail Connor greeted her.

"You're going to the Ladies' Circle meeting today, aren't you? If you'd like to have lunch with Benjamin and me, we can walk to the church together."

Greta had declined all of Abigail's earlier invitations, but that hadn't dissuaded the doctor's wife. "Oh...uh…"

"I made too much. You'd be doing me a favor."

Greta searched for an excuse. Abigail had always been friendly, encouraging Greta to join the Mason family for Sunday lunch or to accompany her on a shopping trip to nearby Greenville, but Greta had found one reason or another to avoid her.

Abigail took advantage of Greta's hesitation. "Come on in. I'll get you a plate." Abigail walked briskly toward the living quarters located at the back of the clinic.

Greta bit her lip and sagged against the wall. Since there was no way out of it, she steeled herself to withstand the hours of awkwardness that faced her. Abigail Connor — blonde, delicate, beautiful Abigail Connor — was everything Greta could never be.

Having no other choice, Greta forced herself to follow. She'd never visited Dr. Connor's living quarters before, but she'd always been curious. The door separating the clinic from the doctor's home had been propped open, revealing a cozy parlor. Greta imagined Dr. Connor and Abigail snuggling in front of the fireplace, talking over the events of the day, and jealousy shot a dart into her heart. She winced from the shame that immediately followed. Jealousy was a sin. A sin that made Greta miserable almost every day.

Beyond the parlor, another open door led to the kitchen. Greta peeked into that room as though she were a timid mouse. It was painted buttercup yellow, a shade that matched Abigail's sunny disposition, and a gentle breeze fluttered lacy white curtains. Dr. Connor sat at a tiny table while Abigail worked at the stove. Greta inched her way into the room, fully expecting someone to rectify the situation and send her on her way.

"Greta," Dr. Connor said, "did Emily O'Keefe say all her children were sick or just the youngest one?"

Hearing no objections, Greta walked to Dr. Connor's chair, took the paper from his outstretched hand, and looked at the list of house calls he had to make that afternoon. "Mrs. O'Keefe only told me about the baby. I didn't know she had other children."

Dr. Connor rubbed his chin. "If she didn't mention them, they're probably fine."

Abigail approached with two plates of food. "Sit down, Greta."

The table was only big enough for two. What about Abigail? Greta glanced at Dr. Connor for help, but he didn't appear to notice her dilemma.

"And Sara Caine," he continued, "needs more medication for her father's gout. He's eighty-four years old. I'm surprised that's all he needs."

"That's all Mrs. Caine asked for," Greta answered, still standing.

Abigail set one plate of food in front of Dr. Connor. He set the paper aside and reached for his wife's hand. "Thank you, Abigail. This looks delicious."

Abigail beamed at him with undisguised love. "Nothing special. Just ham, potatoes, and a smidgen of squash."

He kissed her hand before releasing it. "Abigail knows I'm no lover of squash."

Abigail placed an identical plate in front of the empty chair. "Go ahead and sit down, Greta. I've already eaten."

Greta eased into the straight-backed chair. "My mother boils winter squash and mixes it with brown sugar and butter. Maybe you'd like it that way."

Dr. Connor looked at his wife, and Greta's stomach lurched. She hadn't meant to criticize Abigail's cooking. Why did she always manage to say the wrong thing?

"That sounds delicious," Abigail said. "I'll try it next time."

Greta released her breath, and Dr. Connor returned his attention to the list of patients he planned to visit. He scribbled a few notes and ate absentmindedly while Abigail busied herself at the sink. Greta took a forkful of potatoes, followed by a bite of ham and a morsel of squash. Abigail was a good cook. Not that Greta was surprised. Abigail could do everything with ease.

Jealousy again. Greta rolled her lips inward as she chastised herself. She had to stop envying every married woman she met. Not every marriage was happy, and she'd never heard of a real Prince Charming who could banish her self-doubts with one kiss. But women like

Abigail, pretty, cheerful Abigail, had their pick of men. Women like Greta took what was offered.

When he'd finished eating, Dr. Connor tucked the list of patients into his jacket pocket and stood. "I'd better get on the road. I should be home in time for supper, sweetheart." He kissed Abigail on the cheek.

"I hope so," she replied. "I worry about you driving after dark."

He headed through the door. "See you tomorrow, Greta."

He was gone before she could respond.

"He works so hard," Abigail said, "but he loves it."

"His patients certainly love him," Greta replied. "Every day there's at least one patient who tells me how wonderful Dr. Connor is."

Abigail removed his empty plate and carried it to the sink. "Benjamin says when he first started working in Brightfield, he couldn't keep up with everything. You've helped him a lot."

"That's kind of you to say." Greta carried her plate to the sink. "I love working at the clinic " Without the few hours she spent at the clinic six days a week, she'd have nothing to do. Absolutely nothing.

"I'm going to leave the dishes until tonight," Abigail said. "Just let me get my hat, and I'll be ready to go."

She disappeared down a hallway that Greta assumed led to the bedrooms. Greta scraped the food off the plates and rinsed them off. Her hat and handbag were at her desk, and she returned to the clinic to get them. An unfamiliar lightness filled her chest. Abigail hadn't been insulted by Greta's cooking suggestion, and Dr. Connor had treated her presence at lunch as commonplace. Perhaps she'd be invited to join them again.

And, when she got to the church, Abigail and her mother would probably let Greta sit with them at the Ladies' Circle. When she sat alone, Greta felt like a spotlight was centered on her, calling everyone's attention to the big girl in the corner. But Abigail's mother always took an interest in Greta and made sure she was involved in activities and conversation. Helen Mason never failed to be friendly.

CHAPTER TWO

Henry Mitchell didn't greet George and his father with a shotgun, but he was clearly surprised to see them when he opened his door.

"What brings you out this way?" Henry asked in a gravelly voice as he escorted them to the parlor. "I haven't seen either one of you since the championship game last August."

One mention of baseball, and George's father was soon reliving memorable plays with Henry. George sat back in an armchair and studied the older man. Thick white hair topped a clean-shaven face, and deep lines creased Henry's forehead and eyes. George estimated his age as late fifties to early sixties. Most men who lived that long contented themselves with a rocking chair in front of the fire, but Henry's animated conversation displayed a lively mind.

George looked around the sparsely furnished parlor. Henry had never married, and his simple cottage definitely lacked a woman's touch. No curtains hung in front of the small windows, and only a few landscape prints hung on the wall.

As talk of the baseball game concluded, Henry gestured to the tube George had laid across his knees. "What you got there?"

"Blueprints, Mr. Mitchell," George answered. "I wanted to talk to you about a building project."

Curiosity glinted in Henry's eyes. "I was wonderin' what brought you out here. Come on back to my workroom."

George ducked his head as he followed Henry through an entryway and down a narrow hall. A large, waist-high table filled the room at the end, and large curtainless windows let in ample light. Henry gestured toward the blueprints. "Let's see what you got."

George pried the metal lid from the tube and withdrew the plans. As he rolled out the blueprints, Henry picked up a pail from the floor and produced fist-sized river rocks to use as paperweights. "It's going to be a group of ten houses," George explained, "to replace those shacks near the freight depot." He described the project in detail, including the challenges he faced in completing the job on time.

Henry fished a pair of spectacles from his shirt pocket and slipped them on. He flipped through each sheet of blueprints and bent over the drawings.

George fought his impatience. What did Henry think? Would he be able to help? Would he pronounce George a fool for tackling such a large job?

After several minutes, Henry straightened up and removed his eyeglasses. "What's your budget for ten houses?"

"The landowner gave me twenty thousand to start with "

"Nice," Henry said with a grin. "With that much money you can hire enough men to get the job done quick. What you done so far?"

George hesitated. It was difficult to admit how baffled he was. His father came to his rescue.

"That's what we wanted to talk to you about, Henry. Would you be willing to help George get this done? He could benefit from your advice."

Henry slid his hands into the back pockets of his trousers. "If advice is all you want, I'm ready and able. But my old bones complain if I do too much."

George hurried to reassure the man. "The truth is I don't know where to begin. I started a list of all the things I need to do, but that list is never-ending. Should I hire the men or buy the lumber? Should I store the materials on site or rent a warehouse? And what about the utilities?"

Henry nodded slowly and smiled. "And you're willing to pay me to tell you what to do?"

George's father chuckled. "I know what you're thinking, Henry. Few men like to be bossed around. But George was man enough to admit he needs help, and you're the best man I know to guide him. If you're willing."

A moment of silence passed while Henry appeared to be considering the offer. At last, he extended his hand to George. "Sounds like fun."

***

Greta sat next to Helen Mason, Abigail's mother, in the fellowship hall of Brightfield Christian Church. She enjoyed observing the ladies, sometimes feeling like Sherlock Holmes in her ability to deduce information about the women. This year's leader, for example, always wore the same two dresses to church functions. Sometimes Mrs. Stanton would wear the blue one to Sunday services and the green one on Wednesdays, other weeks the days would be interchanged. One thing was clear — she only had two dresses nice enough for church.

Her husband worked at the Superior Farm Machinery factory in Greenville, but it was rumored most of his paycheck was spent in the tavern. Mrs. Stanton should make arrangements with the paymaster to give the checks directly to her, but she was probably too embarrassed. Greta could certainly understand. She knew a thing or two about keeping secrets.

Lilah Morton sat in the row in front of her. Always dressed in the latest fashion with hats to match, Greta wondered where she could possibly store so many hats. Did her bedroom wall have dozens of hats hanging from nails or did she stack the hatboxes into towering structures like building blocks? Her husband was a lawyer, and her only child was grown and gone, so it was possible Lilah had the funds to lavish on her wardrobe. What she didn't have, however, was the ability to keep a secret. She was well-known as the town's lead gossip. She pounced on every bit of hearsay that crossed her path, never bothering to consider how such rumors might affect the people involved. For all her money, it was a shame Lilah couldn't buy an ounce of empathy.

As the meeting ended, the ladies gathered around the refreshment table for lemonade and cookies. Most of the chatter bored Greta, so she stood on the edge of the group, sipping her lemonade, and listening politely. She usually left once the meeting ended, but Abigail would expect to walk home with her, and Greta couldn't simply disappear.

From the corner of her eye, Greta glimpsed Lilah Morton making her way toward Abigail and Helen. The previous summer, Lilah had spread rumors about Dr. Connor losing interest in Abigail. Now that Abigail was his wife, Greta wondered if Abigail secretly longed to rub Lilah's nose in that fact.

"Aren't you both looking well?" Lilah cooed when she approached. "How is everyone in your family?"

Abigail turned her back to Lilah and rolled her eyes at Greta. Greta stifled a laugh and choked on her lemonade.

Helen was a paragon of civility. "Everyone's fine, Lilah. What do you hear from your son in Chicago?"

"He's doing wonderfully. Already been promoted, don't you know."

Abigail attempted to rescue her mother. "Mom, will you help me in the kitchen? We need to refill the pitchers."

"Of course. Excuse us, Lilah."

As Abigail and her mother retrieved near-empty pitchers from the table, Lilah turned her pernicious attention on Greta. "So nice to see you again. I imagine you have hundreds of stories to tell about Dr. Connor's clinic. Has he been busy?"

Lilah's motive was as clear as glass, but Greta couldn't be tricked into spilling secrets. She'd promised Dr. Connor to keep clinic business confidential. "Dr. Connor is always busy."

Lilah looked around the room as she spoke to Greta. "I'm sure that must be true. If I didn't have such a long history with my doctor in Greenville, I'd visit him. Everyone says it wasn't his fault Mary Grafford died, even though she'd never been sick a day in her life."

Greta silently counted to ten. Mrs. Grafford had been eighty-five years old when she'd suffered an apoplexy. Dr. Connor had been called after she passed away in her sleep. Unable to think of a safe reply, Greta simply smiled.

"Easter will be here before you know it," Lilah continued. "Will your husband be home by then?"

Greta's heart ceased beating, and her breath searched for a hiding place. What did Lilah know? Greta had told the truth, her husband was indeed working in another part of the state, but she hadn't told the whole truth. She never would. "I'm not sure, Mrs. Morton. I certainly hope so."

"It's so unfortunate he couldn't find work close by. What kind of work does he do?"

"He's a salesman for Washburn Flour Mills. My father is a grocer, and that's how we met."

"Isn't that interesting. I imagine he travels all over the country selling his products."

Abigail and her mother returned with the lemonade, and Greta saw her chance to escape. "It was nice speaking with you, Mrs. Morton, but it's time for me to leave." She gave the old gossip a false smile and moved to Abigail's side. "I'd like to leave soon. Do you want me to wait for you?"

"It's up to you," Abigail said. "I need to help Mom clean up, so I may not be ready to leave when you are."

So casual. So sincere. Abigail genuinely didn't care which choice Greta made. "I'll leave then, unless you want help cleaning up."

"No need," Helen Mason said. "Abigail and I can get it done in just a few minutes. But Greta, I wanted to ask if you are free for lunch on Sunday."

There it was again. Did Abigail and her mother pity her? Did they think they could fix her loneliness and solitude by feeding her? "Let me get back to you," Greta answered, even though she would spend every excruciating hour of Sunday afternoon and evening with nothing to do.

"I'll see you tomorrow," Abigail said.

Greta raised her hand in a gesture of farewell and made her way to the door. Maybe it would be wrong to decline Helen's invitation, but Greta had some pride. A pride that evidently kept her from trusting people enough to tell them the truth.

CHAPTER THREE

The hinges squeaked ominously as George and Henry opened the warehouse doors. "How'd you hear about this place?" George asked.

"Belongs to my old boss. It's his widow's property now. Her son says we can lease it for as long as we want."

George scanned the cavernous interior. He could tell without measuring there was plenty of room for lumber, hardware, and the dray wagons or a truck.

"There's a small office this way," Henry said, pointing to the front corner of the building. "Before you know it, you'll be swamped with paper. Receipts from the lumber yard and hardware store, permits from the utility companies, payroll, checklists, schedules. The paperwork is endless."

One corner of the warehouse had been walled off to form space for an office. The bottom section was built with wood, but the top half was a series of windows which allowed the occupants to keep an eye on the warehouse workers. Tall cabinets with multiple drawers lined the back wall and two desks had been pushed together. Thick layers of dust coated the furniture and floated in the shafts of sunlight coming through the grimy windows.

Henry pulled out one of the drawers. "We need to throw out all this old paper to make room for the new."

"If you'll arrange the lease, I'll talk to the lumber yard about our order. We can tear down the empty shacks while we wait for the materials to be delivered."

Henry picked up an empty nail keg. "Sounds good to me. What you goin' to do 'bout transportin' the lumber to the worksite?"

"That's a good question. Which is better, dray wagons and horses or motorized trucks?"

Henry stroked his chin while he thought. "Maybe both. I'm all for modern machinery, but you don't want to have a truck break down on you and no back up plan. There's plenty of farmers 'round here who'll hire out their team and wagon for a fair price. That way, you wouldn't have to worry 'bout takin' care of the animals."

It was the perfect solution. So far, Henry had helped George secure permits for the town's utilities, found a warehouse, and resolved the question of transportation. His father had certainly recommended the right man. "Time to hire some men. Thought I'd start with general laborers and add skilled workers as needed."

Henry pulled out a stack of papers from one of the drawers and stuffed it into the nail keg. "That ought to work. But remember, general laborers aren't likely to have their own tools. Goin' to have to buy some to help with the demolition."

"Already on the list."

"What you plannin' on payin'?"

"I asked around town and found out carpenters, plumbers, and bricklayers are getting seventy-five cents an hour. Laborers should probably get less."

"That would be fair. But skilled workmen can be hard to find. And if they're already on a job, why should they leave it?"

George gazed at the older man, trying to decipher the meaning behind his words. "You think I should offer more?"

"If you want the best. Have you thought about someone to manage the paperwork and payroll?"

"Like who?"

"That's what bookkeepers do."

"Got one of those in your back pocket?"

"Sorry, but the only bookkeeper I know died last year."

George took a deep breath and blew it out. "The list of things I need to do is growing so fast, I don't know what to do first." He reached into his back pocket and withdrew the now-battered notebook.

Henry held out his palm. "Let me see that. If we scrape real hard, maybe the two of us can find enough brains to prioritize that list."

***

On Sunday morning, Greta slipped into the sanctuary of the Brightfield Christian Church. She timed her entry strategically, waiting until the congregation was halfway through the first hymn before she took her usual seat in the back row. She loved Sunday services — the immutable order of worship, the soothing music, the pastor's uplifting message. In church she could feel God's love and acceptance. He'd created her to be tall and strong, able to lift heavy barrels in her father's shop or reach the topmost shelf without a ladder, and surely the Lord was pleased with his creation.

But Greta lived in a world where dainty women were valued. Beauty was defined by delicate features and willowy figures, an ideal she could never fulfill. She'd spent months eating only one meal a day, but her body had refused to shrink. She'd tried different styles of clothing, but nothing hid her height. She knew the pain of no one asking her to dance, and the chagrin of no one bidding on the opportunity to share a picnic meal with her during a church fundraiser. Bit by bit, Greta had learned to hide, until all her spontaneity and joy were locked beneath lessons cruelly taught.

And then Emile Franklin had walked into her father's store.

Greta steeled herself against tears. She'd learned to cry silently, but church was no place for self-pity. Her father and mother had warned her about Emile, and when their ominous predictions had come true, Greta had withdrawn further within herself. Shame fueled her silence, and silence nourished her solitude.

Dr. Connor had shown her how to escape that self-imposed punishment. He'd given her a job, had introduced her to Helen Mason, and had befriended her. She was gradually finding the way back to herself. She could remember the bliss of girlhood, before she'd learned of her flaws, and she could imagine a time when that kind of happiness would be possible. But how did she get to that nebulous future joy?

After the hymn came the prayers, and after the prayers, the sermon. The service ended, and Greta's neighbors greeted each other with smiles and handshakes. Helen reached her first.

"I've been looking for you," Helen said as she laid a gentle hand on Greta's back. "I think it would be best if you rode with Benjamin and Abigail in their automobile. We have the wagon, but it's far from comfortable."

Confused thoughts swam through Greta's mind. What was Helen talking about?

Helen turned around to scan the group of people behind her. "Abigail?"

"Here I am." As the crowd thinned, Abigail's sunny face came into view. "Are you ready, Greta? Benjamin is starving, and he's not very pleasant when he's hungry."

At last the memory surfaced. Sunday lunch with the Masons. Greta had forgotten. "Oh, I don't think —"

Helen ended Greta's refusal by nudging her and Abigail into the flow of departing bodies. "I'll see you at home. Both of you."

The expression on Helen's face was familiar. It was the look all mothers gave when they would not tolerate any dissension. Greta clenched her jaw and followed Abigail.

"I'm so glad you're coming to lunch," Abigail said with a wide smile. "You've worked with Benjamin for seven months, and we still don't know you very well."

Surely Dr. Connor had told his wife why Greta was alone in Brightfield. Doctor-patient confidentiality didn't extend to spouses, did it?

"I hope you've prepared yourself," Abigail continued. "When my whole family gets together, the chaos can be overwhelming." Greta knew the Masons meant well, and she really didn't want to spend another Sunday afternoon and evening in miserable loneliness, but going from solitude to chaos was a big first step. She placed a hand on top of her stomach to quell her prickly nerves.

Dr. Connor stood next to his car, smiling and talking to Abigail's brother, Andrew. Greta could tell Andrew was Abigail's twin, although Abigail was exceedingly feminine, and Andrew was decidedly masculine.

Abigail greeted her brother with a kiss on the cheek. "Did you remember to bring the seed catalogues?"

"Of course not," Andrew replied, "but Hildy did."

"What did I do?"

Greta turned to see the extremely stylish and incredibly beautiful Hildy Campbell approaching. Hildy Mason now, she corrected herself. Andrew had married her a few months earlier.

"You brought the seed catalogues for Mom," Abigail said.

"Hildy, Greta is joining us for Sunday dinner."

"How nice," Hildy said. "Prepare yourself for pandemonium."

Dr. Connor tried to reassure her. "Don't listen to Hildy. It's not as bad as she makes it sound."

Had he discerned her hesitation, or was he simply watching out for one of his patients? He smiled and opened the back door of the automobile for her. "I'll take you home early if it's too much," he said in a voice only she could hear. "But Helen wouldn't have invited you unless she liked you."

Greta climbed into the motorcar. A few minutes later, she, Dr. Connor, and Abigail were bouncing their way down a dirt road toward a large farmhouse.

The Masons' home was a two-story structure, painted white with dark green shutters. A wide porch featuring potted flowers and rocking chairs encircled three sides of the house. Sheets fluttered from a clothesline and brown and white chickens scampered freely around the grassy lawn. It was as homey as hot chocolate and fresh-baked cookies, and Greta wanted to move in immediately.

Abigail turned in her seat and looked at Greta. "We arrived before everyone else."

Dr. Connor opened his wife's door and then Greta's. As they slid out of the automobile, Andrew parked a red-and-white Oldsmobile next to Dr. Connor's Ford.

"Who taught you to drive?" Dr. Connor asked.

A smiling Andrew got out of his motorcar and hurried to open Hildy's door. "My wife, of course. I couldn't keep waiting for you to show me. Hildy's a prettier teacher than you, anyway."

Dr. Connor raised his hands in surrender. "No argument there."

Hildy headed up the wide wooden steps of the porch. "What should we do first, Abigail?"

Abigail followed Hildy but stopped on the bottom step to wait for Greta. Abigail's smile, so patient and welcoming, calmed Greta's misgivings. Everything would be fine. Surely all the Masons would be as warm and kind as Helen and Abigail were.

Hildy held the screen door open so Abigail and Greta could enter. Greta stepped into a parlor designed for family comfort. Several mismatched upholstered chairs and small tables were arranged around a large, open-hearth fireplace. She could easily imagine the family gathered there on winter nights, secure and warm despite a menacing blizzard outside.

Hildy and Abigail removed their hats as they passed through an open doorway adjacent to the parlor. Although fashion dictated that women wear stylish hats, Greta had settled for a small, plain brown one. Fashionable hats decorated with flowers and feathers called attention to herself, and that was the last thing she wanted.

She followed Abigail into a spacious kitchen with a long, rectangular dining table. The tempting aroma of home cooking surrounded Greta and tempted her empty stomach. She was suddenly ravenous. Abigail went to the oven and used potholders to remove a roasting pan.

"How can I help?" Greta asked. She wanted to do something other than stand on the sidelines and feel awkward.

"Want to set the table?" Abigail asked. "We'll be a total of nine. You'll find extra chairs on the sun porch."

Hildy removed mismatched dishes from a cabinet and stacked them on the counter. Within a few minutes, Greta had carried in the extra chairs, set nine places at the table, and poured water into nine tumblers.

The sound of a wagon and Helen's familiar voice indicated the rest of the Mason clan had arrived. "Here they come," Abigail said.

Helen entered the kitchen and seemed to simultaneously remove her hat and put on her apron. "My, my. Looks like you ladies took care of everything."

Hildy set bowls of vegetables and a basket of yeast rolls on the table. Abigail lifted a platter of roasted chicken. "You cooked it, Mom. All we had to do was serve. Who dares tell the hungry coyotes dinner is ready?"

"I will," Hildy said with a laugh. "They don't scare me as much as they used to."

Greta watched Hildy glide out of the kitchen as though she were a swan. How did women do that? Her mother used to complain that Greta walked like a dockworker.

She heard the screen door open followed by Hildy's melodious call. Seconds later, boisterous voices announced the entrance of five men dressed in their Sunday best. The atmosphere in the kitchen seemed to shift. Greta and the other women had worked diligently to ready the food, but the men brought vitality and vigor with them.

"Smells good, Mom," said the oldest Mason son. John was tall like his brother Andrew but had brown hair instead of blond. All the Masons were brunettes except Andrew and Abigail, and Greta wondered if their mother had been a blonde before her hair turned gray.

George Mason also had dark hair, but that's where his resemblance to the family ended. He was easily the tallest man she'd ever seen. He'd removed his jacket, and his broad shoulders and muscular arms seemed to stretch the seams of his white shirt. His face was clean-shaven, but a hint of dark stubble shadowed his cheeks and chin. Greta had seen George and Andrew when they'd renovated Dr. Connor's clinic and living quarters, but she'd never spoken to George. His rugged build and dark looks didn't invite small talk, and she hoped he was as kind as the rest of his family.

There were four open seats, and Greta wondered which one was meant for her. "Over here, Greta," Abigail said. "Come sit next to me."

Greta lowered herself into the straight-backed chair and spread a napkin in her lap. George sat in the chair next to hers. She dared not look at the big man, but from her vantage point she could see his rugged hands. An unbandaged cut bisected three knuckles on his right hand, and she wondered what had happened. If they were at the clinic, she'd know exactly which ointment and gauze to use to dress his injury. But they were at his family home, and she had no business offering to care for him.

When everyone was seated, two chairs remained empty.

"Where's Andrew and Hildy?" Helen asked.

John cupped one hand around his mouth. "Andrew! Stop kissing your new wife and get in here so we can eat!"

A good-natured chuckle passed around the table. "Well, I'm not waiting," Simon Mason said. "Let's say the blessing."

Before they could bow their heads, Andrew and Hildy entered the kitchen, their faces as red as geraniums. "I knew it!" John crowed. "Can't you kiss her at your own house?"

Hildy had several seed catalogs tucked under one arm. She lay them on the kitchen counter and sat in one of the empty chairs.

Andrew put his hand on John's shoulder. "I can, big brother, and I do. But that doesn't stop me from kissing her when no one's around."

"Hear, hear," Dr. Connor said. He slid his arm around Abigail's shoulders and nestled her against him. "We married men know a good thing when we see it."

John dropped his head into his hand. "All right, all right! Can we eat now?"

Another round of laughter passed among the family. Simon took his wife's hand on one side and John's hand on the other. "Let's say the blessing so my first born can enjoy Sunday dinner."

Abigail took Greta's right hand, leaving her no choice but to place her left hand into George's. She tried to concentrate on Simon's brief prayer, but the warm strength of George's calloused palm kindled a curious emotion. Part elation and part serenity, it was a feeling she'd never experienced. When Simon finished the blessing and George withdrew his hand, Greta felt suddenly hollow, as though part of her heart had been snatched away.

Platters and bowls were passed from one person to another as the family served themselves. "Now then," Simon said in a loud voice, "it's time for the weekly report. John, how are things with you?"

John swallowed his food and washed it down with water. "Nothing's new with me. I've been repairing fences and preparing the fields. I'll be planting corn and oats first."

"How is Rosalind?" Abigail asked.

"I haven't seen her since last Sunday. I'll ride over there after dinner."

"How long have you been engaged now?" Abigail asked with raised eyebrows.

"Not that it's any of your business," John said in an annoyed tone, "but it will be a year in June."

A year-long engagement didn't seem excessive, but the uncomfortable silence following John's statement told Greta he resented Abigail's question.

Simon shifted his gaze to his daughter. "Abigail? Benjamin? What's your news?"

Dr. Connor wiped his mouth with a napkin. "The clinic has been busier than ever, but the warmer weather should help end the influenza cases."

"Nothing's new with me, Dad," Abigail answered.

Abigail's father raised his chin and eyebrows. "I keep hoping either you or Hildy will have news about my first grandchild."

"Mr. Mason," Hildy said in a censorious tone, "I've only been married a few months! Don't rush me."

Simon laughed and gestured to the next person. "Andrew, I heard you were on your way to the state capital."

Andrew wiped his mouth with his napkin. "Yes sir. The legislature's in session, and I've been assigned to cover our representatives."

"You're not becoming one of the muckrakers, are you?" Simon asked.

Andrew grinned and shook his head. "I certainly hope not. My goal is to keep my ears and eyes open and report only facts."

Abigail leaned forward to look at Andrew. "Just wait until women get the vote. That will shake up the government."

John groaned loudly. "Not this again. Can't we have one meal without arguing about women's suffrage?"

Abigail opened her mouth to respond, but Simon held up a staying hand. "Not now, daughter. You're not going to change anyone's mind at this table, and we have a guest. I believe Mrs. Franklin would enjoy her meal more if we didn't have another political argument."

Abigail's expression clearly showed her discontent, but she obeyed her father's wishes.

Simon pointed his fork at Andrew's wife. "All right, Hildy, since I'm not allowed to ask about grandchildren, what news do you have?"

Hildy smiled warmly at her father-in-law. "I wish to yield my turn because I'm anxious to hear from George."

All gazes turned to the big man sitting next to Greta. George placed his fork and knife on the table and sat back in his chair. "Like I told you last Sunday, my construction company is still taking shape. I rented a warehouse over on Jefferson Street, and I spoke to Otto Claywell about hiring his team of Belgians." The hint of a smile curved George's lips. "Old Otto acted like I'd offered him a pot of gold. He promised he'd deliver them hitched to his dray wagon every morning and pick them up every night."

"Otto's been trying to sell those horses and wagon for six months," John explained. "Hiring them out to you is almost as good."

"Doesn't matter to me," George continued, "and this way I don't have to feed and care for the animals."

George didn't elaborate, so his mother prompted him. "What else, son?"

"I ordered the lumber for the first house and warned Aaron Turner at the lumber yard there are nine more houses to come."

"What did Aaron say?" asked Simon

George's grin widened. "Not much. He just sort of danced a jig. Then I ordered tools from Jasper Lewis at the hardware store."

"Did Jasper dance too?" John asked.

"No, but I did hear him whistling while he wrote up the order."

The Mason family laughed. Greta enjoyed listening to George's deep voice. He had a storyteller's way of recounting his actions that held her attention.

"Sounds like you're making the whole town richer and happier," Simon remarked. "What's next?"

George rubbed the side of his face with his palm. "Hiring the workmen, I suppose. I put a notice in the *Brightfield Gazette* that I'd be hiring tomorrow morning. I know a lot of the skilled laborers already, but Henry Mitchell says I need a bookkeeper. Any of you know a good one?"

Dr. Connor folded his napkin and placed it on the table. "I know a very good one, but you can't have mine."

Greta's face warmed. Until that moment, no one had paid attention to her. But when both Abigail and Dr. Connor turned their smiles on her, so did everyone else.

George lowered his head to look at her. "I know you work in Benjamin's office, but I didn't know you were a bookkeeper."

"She's the best," Dr. Connor said. "Greta, if you're interested in helping George get his business started, I won't object, but please don't leave me in the lurch."

"I would never do that," Greta managed to say.

"But she only works half a day," Abigail explained to George. "We don't want to keep her from earning more money if she can."

George shifted in his chair so he could face her. "Well, Mrs. Franklin, I don't want to get in trouble with my brother-in-law, but I could sure use some help. I can match whatever Benjamin's paying you."

Greta wanted to jump at the opportunity, but she'd learned the hard way that committing to something without knowing the details was a dangerous gamble. "I'd like to know more before I take you up on your offer."

Before George could reply, Abigail asked a question. "Is your warehouse that big building on the corner of Jefferson and Pierce?"

George shifted his gaze to his sister. "That's it. Across the street from the machine shop."

Abigail touched Greta's arm. "If it's all right with you, we'll walk over there tomorrow after the clinic closes. You can look around and talk to George."

"Henry Mitchell will be there," George said to her. "He has about thirty years of experience in the construction business, and he's been advising me."

Greta could decline George's offer, invent some credible reason why working with him would be too difficult, but she was intrigued by the possibility. Her lonely afternoons would be filled, she'd double her income, and her skills were needed. In a world where awkwardness shadowed her day and night, being needed was a powerful weapon against self-doubt.

Greta turned to Abigail. "Sounds like a good idea."

George turned toward Dr. Connor. "Don't worry, Benjamin. Even though Mrs. Franklin will prefer working with me, I'm sure she'll give you time to find another bookkeeper."

Greta started to object, but the family laughed at George's claim. She smiled in relief at the realization George had been joking. The Mason family clearly loved each other, and good-natured teasing was one way they showed it.

***

George pushed away from his plate and looked at his family. In the last six months, he had acquired a brother-in-law and a sister-in-law, but they had been woven into the fabric of his family so well, it was difficult to think of them as ever being separate. Greta's uneasiness had been apparent, but when his mother and sister had included her in the family's conversation, she'd relaxed a few degrees.

Once the meal was finished, the women began to clear the table. Greta stood and carried two dirty plates to the sink. "Thank you," George's mother said as she filled the sink with water. "Why don't you go out to the porch with the others? We'll get this done in a flash."

George fixed his gaze on Greta. How would she react to his mother's well-intentioned dismissal? His mother had meant to excuse Greta from an irksome chore, but Greta would probably prefer to wash dishes than sit outside with the men.

"Mrs. Franklin, do you like kittens?" he asked.

Greta turned toward him, an expression of bewilderment on her face. "Kittens?"

"Our barn cat had a litter. They're about two weeks old, and I thought you might like to see them."

Greta turned her gaze to Abigail who was scraping leftover food into a bin.

"Go ahead," his mother said, "and take some of the leftover chicken to the mother cat."

Abigail handed a bowl of chopped meat to Greta. "I'll join you when I finish here."

Greta held the bowl against her stomach and looked at George as though she were trying to decide. He went to the back door and opened

30

it for her. She moved quietly, her gaze on his face, until she descended the steps and stood in the spring sunshine.

"This way," George said, gesturing with his arm.

She walked beside him, silent and watchful, like a soldier on sentry duty. He was accustomed to women being wary of him. Although he tried to always be polite and friendly, his size threatened many people. But Greta was no petite flower. The top of her head reached his shoulder, and her shoulders were broad and straight. In another time, she could have easily managed a milkmaid's yoke. Her legs must be long and powerful, but he couldn't see much beneath the simple wool skirt she wore.

He'd been fascinated by her since she first caught his eye. Many women had pretty faces, but Greta had a powerful beauty. Reddish-brown hair framed pale skin, and her dark eyes sparkled with intelligence. She belonged on the prow of a sailing ship, breaking the waves of uncharted seas and protecting sailors from mythical monsters. Instead, she wore sensible business suits and worked in Benjamin's clinic.

Worst of all, she was a married woman.

That piece of information had stopped George from pursuing Greta, but not from admiring her. He'd seen her often at church, but he'd never seen her husband. Abigail had told him Greta's husband was a salesman who was usually on the road, but the mysterious Mr. Franklin never came home. How could a man stay away from a woman like Greta?

She paused at the entrance to the barn and glanced at George. "The momma cat's made a nest for her family over here," he said, stepping toward an empty stall.

The sound of mewling kittens greeted him as he led her to the mound of straw in the corner. The mother cat, a tabby with gray and black stripes, hissed at George as he squatted near her kittens.

"It's all right, Little Momma," he said in a soothing tone. "Nobody's going to hurt your babies."

All of Greta's previous uneasiness seemed to evaporate as she knelt beside George. "Oh," she sighed in a reverential whisper, "how precious "

"Hand me the food."

Greta passed the bowl of chicken without taking her gaze from the kittens.

George set the bowl a few feet away from the nest. Instantly curious, the mother cat sprang to her feet. She sniffed briefly and then crouched down to enjoy her treat. "Is there a kitten you fancy, Mrs. Franklin?"

Greta placed one hand on her stomach and the other on her throat. "Oh, I can't take one. I live in the boarding house, and I doubt the landlady would let me have a cat."

"They're too young to leave their mother now," George explained. "What I meant is, which one would you like to hold?"

A hesitant smile teased Greta's lips. "Sure their mother won't mind?"

"She's distracted for the moment." George wrapped his large hand around one of the tiny babies and lifted it from the straw. "Here you go." He deposited the kitten in her palm.

"Oh," Greta cooed, "aren't you just the sweetest thing?" She cuddled the cat against her chest and stroked its head with her forefinger. "Yes, you are. Pretty soon you'll be ready to explore this barn and the rest of the world, but for now, you stay close to momma."

The kitten bumped its nose against Greta's finger and emitted a tiny sound. The mother cat leaped from the bowl to Greta's lap and fastened her teeth around the scruff of her baby's neck.

"They're definitely too young to leave their mother," Greta said as she watched the mother cat carry the baby back to the nest. "Or at least, the mother's not ready for them to leave."

"It seems to me," George said as he eased into a sitting position, "people either prefer dogs or cats or neither. Which are you?"

"I like both, actually. Why put all my love on one animal when I have so much to spread around?"

"I like that answer. Warm-hearted people are my favorite kind."

Greta ducked her head and looked at him through her lashes.

George returned her gaze, unable to stop a grin from curling his lips. Not only was Greta an unusual beauty, she was also tender and loving. Did her husband realize what a lucky man he was?

Emotion charged the silence stretching between them. George yearned to touch her, to take her hand or pull her into an embrace, but this was the first time they had spoken to each other.

Another kitten, this one more gray than black, boldly stepped away from its litter mates and approached Greta. She smiled at the stumbling baby and laid her hand, palm up, on the straw. The kitten investigated her hand with its nose, and then rubbed its face against her palm.

Greta laughed quietly. "You're tickling me," she said to the kitten.

"I think that one just chose you," George said. "I've always heard cats choose their owners."

"I don't know," Greta replied. "My heart wants to say yes, but my head says I'd better talk to the landlady."

"It will be at least a month before the kittens are ready to leave their mother. Think you could talk her into it by then?"

Greta looked up at him. "I'll think about it."

The way she looked at him, one part shy and one part daring, would linger in his memory. Why hadn't he found her first? The fact she was married to someone else burrowed into his conscience like a determined tick.

Greta used one finger to stroke the gray kitten. "What would be a good name for this one?"

George shrugged one shoulder. "Naming rights belong to the owner. The last house cat we had was called Ginger because of her color, but that wouldn't fit this little one."

Greta pursed her lips in thought. "I'll have to think of things that are gray."

"Does that mean you'll take it, Mrs. Franklin?"

"No." She flashed him a quick smile that melted his heart. "And I wish you would call me Greta. No one calls me by my husband's name."

It was the perfect opening for George to ask about that invisible husband of hers. "I've never met your husband. Is he —"

"Greta? George?"

George swallowed the bad word that sprang to his lips. Abigail had picked the exact wrong time to interrupt.

"In the stall," Greta called.

Abigail swung open the stall door, and the light gray kitten rejoined its siblings with one leap. "Oh!" she exclaimed with a laugh. "Look at those sweet things! Has the mother cat let you pick them up?"

"You'd be better off just looking today," George answered.

"Maybe Momma Cat will be less protective next week."

Abigail got on all fours and crawled toward the kittens. "Benjamin said I could take one home. That dark one with the yellow eyes sure is a cutie. And look at that light gray one."

"That one has already laid claim to Greta," George explained.

Abigail looked up at Greta. "Is that right?"

Greta leaned her head toward George. "Your brother is trying to convince me to take one, but I haven't decided."

"Wouldn't it be fun to have them at the clinic?" Abigail asked with a sparkle in her eye. "They could entertain the children."

"And scratch them when the kids pull their tails," George warned.

Abigail made a face at her brother and turned toward Greta. "Anyway ... Benjamin is ready to go. Would you like a ride home?"

"Of course." Greta got to her feet.

George scrambled to stand. "If you'd like to visit longer, I'd be glad to take you home in the buggy."

Greta offered her hand to Abigail and pulled her to a standing position. "Thanks but, I might as well go now."

Abigail led Greta out the stall door. "We'll see you tomorrow, big brother."

George watched his sister and Greta walk side-by-side toward the farmhouse. He'd liked everything he'd seen and learned about his future bookkeeper, and he planned to get to know her a lot better. Most of all, he wanted to get to the bottom of that mystery husband of hers.

CHAPTER FOUR

Although George arrived at his new office early Monday morning, a line of men dressed in overalls and work clothes waited for him. "Morning. You men here about the notice in the paper?"

The men removed their hats, shook his hand, and introduced themselves, but George didn't try to remember their names. He needed to write down the information in the new yellow notebook he'd purchased. "Come on inside," he said to the job seekers.

George swung open the warehouse doors and led the men toward the corner office. They formed an orderly line and waited in silence while George got ready. He'd already hired the men he knew from previous jobs, but in addition to skilled workers, he needed unskilled laborers who could demolish the existing shacks, load the debris into a wagon, and haul it to the burn site on his father's farm.

He sat behind one of the desks and gestured for the first man to enter. "Name?" George asked.

"Vincent Dowling."

The man appeared to be in his thirties, lean and dark-skinned.

He pulled off his cap and held it in front of him, giving George an opportunity to examine the applicant's hands. Dowling's knuckles were enlarged, and several small scars cut across the back of his fingers. They were a working man's hands - just what George was looking for. "Do you have any construction skills?"

"General carpentry and painting."

"Do you have your own tools?"

"Yes, sir."

"The worksite is behind the freight depot. Be there Wednesday morning at eight o'clock. I'm paying a dollar an hour for skilled tradesmen, seventy-five cents an hour for laborers. How does that sound?"

Dowling broke into a wide smile. He jumped to his feet and pumped George's hand. "That sounds like the answer to a prayer. I'll be there Wednesday morning, you'll see. Yes, sir. A dollar an hour. Thank you, sir."

George smiled at the man's enthusiasm. He'd given men jobs before, but they had always been piece work — a few dollars for a bricklayer or a painter. Now he could hire men for permanent positions. Having that potential made his business more important than ever. If George could land another contract once he finished Hildy's houses, he could keep paying his workers. But if he failed, the men would be out of work.

Vincent Dowling walked to the door, stopped, and turned back to say something. "Just so you know, I live in one of those shacks you're going to replace. My wife's really looking forward to moving."

George's newest employee walked out, and the next applicant entered. George took down each man's information and hired everyone who needed a job. By the time he'd reached the end of the line, his stomach growled, and his head ached. Time for lunch.

He stepped outside to fetch the metal pail he used to carry his food and saw Abigail and Greta waiting to cross the road. Why were they so early? He pulled his watch from his vest pocket and shook his head in wonder. Had he really spent five hours hiring workers?

"Hello, big brother," Abigail said as she approached. "How was your morning?"

"Busy. I hired twenty-two workers and forgot to eat lunch."

"Uh-oh," Abigail said with a grin. "Watch out, Greta. When George is hungry, it's easy to mistake him for a bear."

George looked at Greta, afraid she wouldn't realize his sister was teasing, but Greta only grinned. "I might be a bear, but I'm willing to share," George answered. "Come inside, and I'll show you my new office." He retrieved his lunch pail from the wagon and led them into the warehouse.

"My goodness," Abigail said as she looked around the space. "This is the size of two or three barns put together."

George delighted in his sister's appreciation. "I'm going to need it. I have ten houses to build. That's a lot of lumber and a lot of hardware."

"Where would Greta work?"

"This way," George said, gesturing with his arm. He'd planned to eat while they looked around, but as he moved toward the office space, Henry Mitchell walked through the warehouse door.

"Hello there," Henry said with a wide smile. "Didn't know we were expectin' company."

"Do you know my sister?" George asked.

"Met her about fifteen years ago. She's changed a mite since then."

Abigail laughed and shook Henry's hand. "I certainly hope so."

"And I read about her winnin' the baseball game last summer," Henry added with a gleam in his eye.

George shook his head. "She didn't win it all by herself you know."

"Pay him no mind, Mr. Mitchell," Abigail said. "He's just jealous."

"And hungry," Greta added.

"Speaking of lunch," George said, "let's go into the office." He opened the door and waited for the others to enter. "Henry, this is Mrs. Greta Franklin. She might help us with the bookkeeping."

"Good to know," Henry said. "We definitely need one."

"This place is filthy," Abigail said with a scowl.

"We'll get it cleaned up," George promised. "We just haven't had time. But I did empty all the filing cabinets." He opened one of the drawers to show the dust-filled space. "Sit down, everybody. Greta, one of these desks will be for you."

She pulled a wooden chair close to a desk and sat down. "We can move the furniture any way you like," he said. "And I'll get everything organized."

"I can do it," Greta said. "That way I'll know where everything is."

"I'll help you," Abigail volunteered.

One less thing for George. "Well, it's not part of being a bookkeeper, but I'd sure appreciate it."

"We'll clean it together," Abigail said, "and it'll get done a lot faster."

"Now, Greta, what supplies should I buy for a bookkeeper?"

George removed his original blue notebook from a desk drawer and opened it to a clean page.

"Do you have receipts for the materials you've bought?" Greta asked.

"I sure do." George opened another drawer and pulled out papers of various sizes and colors. When he finished, the collection of loose papers resembled the pile of straw the mother cat had formed for her babies. He was seldom embarrassed, but his inability to organize his papers was threatening to turn his face red.

Greta must have seen his discomfort. "Don't worry. Dr. Connor's desk was worse than yours."

Henry and Abigail chuckled, and the tension evaporated. George was already interested in Greta, but that show of empathy increased his attraction tenfold.

"I imagine you have a bank account," Greta said. "Did they give you a book of checks?"

"I'm picking it up this afternoon," George answered. "Should I have your name added to the account?"

Greta's eyes widened. "No, no! You should never do that. Make sure you're the only one who can access your money."

George glanced at Henry who was leaning on the counter, a satisfied smile on his face. "Good advice," Henry said.

Greta had just shown her honesty. She could have easily taken advantage of George's lack of experience, but her innate integrity was obvious.

"How many workers did you hire today?" Henry asked.

"Twenty-two."

Henry whistled. "Goin' to be hard to keep 'em all busy."

"Maybe at the beginning," George said, "but once we get going, we'll have one crew for building and another crew for demolition."

"That means you'll need payroll records," Greta explained.

George looked at Henry. "You weren't joking about needing a bookkeeper."

"Your new bookkeeper's goin' to need supplies," Henry replied. "You'd better open an account at Goodson's stationery store."

George flipped open the blue notebook and added a line to the list of items he needed to accomplish. "I'll take care of it." Then he looked at Greta. "Please tell me you're ready to take this on."

Abigail spoke up. "You haven't told her how much you'll pay."

"Yes, I did," George retorted. "Yesterday, I said I'd pay whatever Benjamin pays."

"What do you think, Greta? Is that enough for you to take on my brother?" Abigail asked.

Greta reached across the desk, gathered the receipts, and placed them in neat stacks. "I'm looking forward to it. May I start tomorrow?"

George clapped his hands together. "Yes, ma'am! Please!"

Laughter rang through the office. Greta's smile lit her face and enhanced her beauty. George liked making Greta smile. He wished he had the right to make her smile every day.

"All right then," Henry said, clasping his hands together. "We'd better get started on your list."

"I'm not leaving until I've eaten," George said. "My stomach thinks I've forgotten it."

"Tell you what," Henry replied. "You eat your lunch, and I'll escort these lovely ladies home."

Greta stood. "Leave these receipts for now. I'll go to the stationery store tomorrow and buy some ledger books and supplies. Then I'll come by to clean and set up the office."

George held up his new yellow notebook. "The names of the men I hired and their pay are written in this notebook. Should I leave it with you?"

"Yes," Greta answered, "I'll get the payroll ledger started right away."

George looked at Henry and grinned. "Now I feel as though I'm running a real business."

"What did you think you were doin' before?" Henry asked.

"Running as fast as I could in a dense fog."

Henry grinned and laid his hand on George's shoulder. "It'll get easier. The first time you do somethin' is always the hardest. Ladies, are you ready to leave?"

"I am," answered Abigail. Greta merely nodded.

Henry opened the door and waited for the ladies to pass through. "Good work today," he said once Abigail and Greta were too far to hear. "You found us a first-rate bookkeeper."

George fell into a chair and reached for the sandwiches he'd made that morning. Henry didn't know it, but as far as George was concerned, Greta was a first rate everything.

***

Greta's spirits lifted during the next few weeks. Her mornings at the clinic bustled with Dr. Connor's clients and his thriving medical practice. Despite her earlier reluctance, she shared lunch with Abigail and Dr. Connor most days and then walked to the warehouse.

Concerned about her safety when working alone, George had put a lock on the office door. As she let herself into the office one afternoon, Greta wondered what he was protecting her from. She didn't mind working alone and being in charge of so many important details encouraged her. Because of her, George knew exactly how much money he had in the bank. Because of her, he didn't worry about which bills had been paid or if Friday's payroll was ready.

She seldom saw him, but almost every day she found a note on her desk with instructions or questions. His handwriting was masculine, his messages brief and to the point. But he always remembered to thank her or give her a brief compliment. She'd never heard her father compliment her mother, and Emile had never thanked her for the many meals she'd prepared or the shirts she'd mended. George was unlike any man she knew, both in appearance and actions, and she was falling in love with him.

It was ridiculous. And hopeless. Nevertheless, her heart refused to be rational. Yes, she was a married woman. Yes, George had shown no more than friendly respect for her. But he embodied everything she'd dreamed of. His physique was her ideal — a big man, obviously strong enough to lift heavy loads, who was also gentle enough to handle kittens. He treated his workers fairly, changing them from laborers to skilled tradesmen based on the quality of their work. For all his concerns, he'd been thoughtful enough to leave her encouraging notes. When she imagined herself with George, she never felt awkward or unwanted. He would make a perfect mate for her, but she hadn't waited.

Of course, she'd never have met George if she hadn't come to Brightfield with her husband. Emile hadn't fulfilled any of her criteria for a husband, except one. He'd proposed. After a lifetime of being overlooked and rejected, she was certain no one else would ask.

The sound of horses and a wagon outside the warehouse redirected her attention. Henry Mitchell entered, found a ladder, and carried it outside. George entered next and walked directly toward the office. Greta sprang from her chair and hurried to open the locked door.

"I'm glad you're here," George said with a wide smile. "Come outside and see what I've got."

Greta's curiosity was piqued. She'd seen him exhausted from work and burdened with concerns, but she'd never seen him as excited as a young boy on Christmas morning. For just a second, she was tempted to wrap her arms around his waist and bury her face into his chest, but she brushed it away and walked beside him through the main entrance.

Two ladders stood on either side of the wide doorway. Henry Mitchell balanced at the top of one, and a man she didn't recognize perched on the other. Between them stretched a large wooden sign.

Rectangular in shape, the top half was red, and the bottom half was blue. The words *Mason Construction* were painted in white block letters. "Oh George," Greta said, "it's beautiful "

George pulled his shoulders back and pushed his chest out. "You think so?"

How odd a confident man like George would want her approval. She put a note of enthusiasm in her reply. "It looks great up there. People will be able to see it from the end of the street."

He slid his hands into his back pockets and gazed at the sign.

"The first house will be finished soon. Would you like to see it?"

Greta suspected he'd be crestfallen if she declined, but she was genuinely eager to see the project that kept him so busy. "Of course! All those blueprints in the office must mean something. I'd love to see how it turned out."

His smile grew wider. "All right, then. If this good weather holds, we'll finish ahead of schedule."

"George!" Henry shouted from atop his ladder. "This bracket is cracked. See if we've got something else that will secure this sign."

"Be right back," he said to Greta before returning to the warehouse.

While she waited, she mentally reviewed the tasks she needed to complete that day. Ten payments to suppliers awaited George's signature. Best to get that done before another chore whisked him away.

She could hear George sorting pieces of hardware as she neared the doorway. "George, before you leave—"

"Watch out!" Henry yelled.

Greta heard Henry's warning and the ominous crack of metal breaking, but her body froze with indecision. Where was the danger? Which way should she move?

Someone pushed her against the wall just as the sign fell from one side and swung like a pendulum. The weight of the free-hanging side tore the remaining bracket and the sign clattered to the ground.

Henry cursed loudly. "Everybody all right down there?" he asked as he descended the ladder.

George's quiet voice sounded in Greta's ear. "Are you hurt?"

Greta blinked. George had pushed her out of the way, and his body, his large, powerfully built body, was wedged against hers. Everyone said Greta was too tall, but George was taller. Everyone said Greta was too broad at the shoulders and hips, but George dwarfed her. His scent enveloped her, and her knees weakened. She'd never felt safer or more feminine than she did at that moment.

"Greta," he repeated, "are you hurt?"

"N-no," she managed to say. "Are *you* hurt?"

She felt his laugh rumble through his chest. "I'm fine," he said and stepped away from her.

A sense of loss replaced his warm protection, and she struggled against holding him in place. But George had apparently been unaffected. He climbed the ladder and inspected the broken bracket as if nothing special had happened.

Greta took a deep breath and let it out. If he could casually return to work so could she. She returned to her desk and tried to focus on a column of numbers in the ledger. She'd always been able to add and subtract quickly and accurately, but at that moment her internal organs were quivering like a candle flame.

She needed to calm down and regain control of her body. She was a married woman. A married woman with a derelict husband, but married, nonetheless. She could dream about George Mason and sustain herself with memories of his body pressed against hers, but nothing would come of it. Nothing except yearning and regrets.

*****

Violet and pink clouds stretched across the evening sky as George knocked on his sister's door. It had been another long day full of problems to solve and conflicts to reconcile, and his body needed to rest. But George couldn't go one hour more without an answer.

Abigail opened the door, her eyebrows raised in surprise. "Hello there, big brother. Everything all right?"

"I'd like to speak to Benjamin. Is he here?"

"He just sat down to dinner. Come on in, and I'll fix you a plate."

George stepped into Abigail's tiny kitchen. "Sorry to interrupt your dinner."

Benjamin sat at their small, square table. "You're always welcome. Grab a chair and tell me what brings you to our house."

George sat across from Benjamin, and Abigail put a plate of chicken and green beans in front of him. "Thanks. Guess you could hear my stomach growling from outside."

"One thing I know about you, big brother," Abigail said with a glint in her eye, "is you're always hungry."

"I used to be like that when I was growing up, but I'm pretty sure I've grown all I'm going to."

"How old are you now?" Benjamin asked.

"Twenty-eight."

"Well, for what it's worth, my medical opinion is you've definitely finished growing."

"Thank goodness," Abigail said. "He's almost a giant now."

George had been teased about his size as long as he could remember, so his sister's gentle badgering had no effect.

"Anything special on your mind?" Benjamin asked.

George laid his knife and fork on the plate and looked squarely at Benjamin. "I need to know more about Greta."

Abigail frowned in apparent confusion. "Greta told me she loved working for you. What's wrong?"

George focused on Abigail. "Did she use those words? She *loved* working for me?"

Abigail gazed at the ceiling. "I think that's what she said." She shifted her gaze to George. "Is it important?"

George drank deeply from a glass of water to buy a few seconds of time. He wasn't one to talk freely about his emotions, but today, after he'd come so close to kissing Greta, he had to get some answers. "I'm interested in her, and I have some questions."

Abigail and Benjamin looked at each other and then at George. "You're interested how?" Abigail asked.

George's stomach tightened at the realization he needed to be more transparent, but he'd come for answers, and being reticent wouldn't get him what he needed. He braced himself for the jokes that would surely follow when he answered truthfully. "Romantically interested. All right?"

Abigail didn't tease or ridicule him. His brothers would have, but his sister had a kinder nature. "I think that's wonderful," she said. "I like Greta very much."

George glanced at Benjamin, wondering how he would react.

"Fine with me, George," Benjamin said. "But she is a married woman."

"That," George said, placing his index finger on the table, "is what I want to know. Is she really married, or does she have a reason to pretend to be married? I asked around, and no one has ever seen her husband."

"Why would she pretend to be married?" Abigail asked.

"Sometimes a woman will invent a husband if she's expecting a baby without the benefit of a wedding. I've also heard of women who pretend to be married because they ran away from their parents and are trying to live under a false identity."

"Well," Abigail answered, "she's not expecting a baby. She's been working for Benjamin since last summer so, if there were a baby, we'd know it by now. I overheard her tell the ladies at church that her father owns a grocery store, and her husband is a salesman."

George turned his attention to Benjamin. "You're awfully quiet. Do you know anything about Greta's husband?"

Benjamin placed his napkin beside his plate and pushed his chair away from the table. "I believe Greta is truly married, but I'm not at liberty to divulge more information about her."

"What does that mean?"

"Greta first came to me as a patient, and my ethics compel me to keep other facts confidential."

George wanted to pounce on any morsel of information. Surely, Benjamin could be persuaded to tell more. "You know something about her husband, don't you?"

Benjamin folded his hands in his lap, as though he held a secret. "I'm sorry, George, but I can't answer your questions."

George's patience was close to snapping, and his jaw ached from clenching his teeth. He knew Benjamin to be a man of his word and arguing with him would be futile.

"Have you asked Greta?"

For a second, George wasn't sure who had asked him the question. Then Abigail laid her hand atop his fist. He forced his hand to relax. Neither his sister nor her husband was responsible for his feelings. Acting on his attraction to Greta was up to him and no one else.

"I know talking to Greta is unavoidable," George admitted, "but I don't want to make her uneasy. If I tell her I'm interested in courting her, she might quit working for me. Then she'd be out of a job, and I'd be out a bookkeeper."

Neither Abigail nor Benjamin offered more advice or comments. George ate the rest of his food while they talked about their day and cleaned the kitchen. Everything about his sister and her husband seemed easy. They spoke in relaxed tones, often finishing each other's sentences. Abigail touched Benjamin frequently, a hand on his arm or a quick embrace, and Benjamin listened, his responses reflecting the comfort they'd found with each other.

How had they reached such ease with each other? George was guilty of not thinking about his sister when she'd been at home. She was the youngest and only girl, and, as youngsters, George had often been irritated by the little sister who had always wanted to tag along with her brothers. She had always simply been there, working alongside his mother and giving as good as she got from her brothers.

Now he saw his little sister with fresh eyes. While he hadn't been paying attention, Abigail had fallen in love and married. Contentment shone through her like sunlight through stained glass.

When he'd finished his food, George thanked his sister and said his goodbyes. He hadn't received the answers he'd sought, but his feelings for Greta wouldn't dim. The only way to resolve the question was to talk to her. And the sooner the better.

CHAPTER FIVE

Easter Sunday dawned with all the perfection spring could muster. The gentle breeze carried the aroma of freshly turned soil, a signal the farmers of Brightfield were preparing their fields for planting. Pale green leaves budded on oaks, and crocus and snowdrops pushed through the warming earth.

As she walked to church that morning, Greta's body felt as though it was experiencing its own awakening. Her legs wanted to run, her arms wanted to dance, and her heart wanted to explode with the love she harbored for George Mason.

Her feelings were impossible, but they flourished, nonetheless. He thought of her as an employee, but, in her fantasies, he was her protector and, most of all, her friend. What harm did it do to dream? As long as she behaved in an upright manner, no one would know the flights of fancy her heart dared. She'd become quite adept at keeping a secret and hiding her love for George would not be a challenge.

At church, she assisted with the youngsters' class, helping them create paper Easter lilies. The congregation was singing the first hymn as she made her way to the sanctuary. As was her habit, she planned to slide into the back row unnoticed.

But as she approached the entrance, her usually confident steps stumbled to a halt. There stood George, dressed in his dark blue Sunday suit. Why wasn't he sitting with his family the way he always did? If she backtracked, perhaps she could leave before he saw her.

The smile he sent her way made it clear there was no escaping.

"Good morning. I've been waiting for you."

Greta swallowed the excitement bubbling in her chest. There was a good chance he just wanted to tell her something about work. "W-W-Why?" She squeezed her eyes shut against the embarrassment that threatened to engulf her. When had she turned into a stuttering twelve-year-old?

George walked slowly toward her. "Because I have two questions for you. First, will you let me sit with you today? And second, would you like to have lunch with my family again?"

Not questions about work after all. "That would be nice. Thank you."

He held his arm out in an invitation for her to go first. They entered the sanctuary and found two vacant seats as the minister read the week's announcements. Greta tried to concentrate on the minister's words, but, with George only inches away, her thoughts fluttered from one forbidden place to another. What would his kiss feel like? If he pulled her close, would he crush her with his strength or caress her like he had the kitten? What would it feel like to have his arms around her as she slept?

But after each illicit fancy, the cold truth crashed her fantasies. It was possible George had his heart set on another woman. Perhaps he valued her bookkeeping skills but nothing else. And the most bitter truth of all, she was a married woman. Her only choice was divorce, and a divorced woman brought shame to a man's family. Something she would never do to the Masons.

Before she knew it, the minister was giving the benediction. As the congregants drifted toward the exit, George was hailed by friends and acquaintances. He introduced Greta to each, although she couldn't recall any names after the sixth one. They finally made their way outside.

George led her to Dr. Connor's automobile where Abigail stood by the driver's door. "I'm glad you're coming to lunch," she said with her usual friendly smile.

"It's nice to be invited," Greta answered before crawling into the rear seat of Dr. Connor's Model F Ford. While she arranged her skirt, George wedged himself into the small space beside her. With his knees against his chin and his elbows pressed against his ribs, he looked miserably cramped.

"Wouldn't you be more comfortable in another motorcar or your family's wagon?" Greta asked.

George shrugged. "It's not far to our house. Otherwise, I'd take your suggestion."

"You look like a folded paper fan."

"I feel like one too."

She laughed then, and George joined her. Why would he put himself in such discomfort just to ride beside her?

Dr. Connor opened the passenger's door for his wife. One look, and Abigail took pity on her brother. "George, there's more space in the front seat. Would you like to trade with me?"

George looked at Greta. "Would you mind?"

"No," she answered. "In fact, I insist on it."

It was almost as difficult for George to disentangle himself as it had been to squeeze into the rear seat, but once everyone was situated, Dr. Connor drove to the Masons' farm.

Greta's nerves were calmer this time. She knew the routine and was welcomed by everyone. She'd surrendered to Abigail's determined kindness and had come to think of her as a friend rather than as Dr. Connor's perfect wife.

Hildy was another matter. Greta had heard that Hildy was the richest woman in town, and her wardrobe certainly supported the rumor. Abigail and her mother made their own clothing, but Hildy obviously bought her elegant gowns from the best fashion houses. They fit her slender body as though they'd been made specifically for her, and each ensemble had matching gloves and wondrous hats. But Hildy had married Andrew Mason and was treated as a member of the family. No one paid attention to her extraordinary appearance. They simply accepted her as she was.

The men had removed their jackets, and some had rolled their shirt sleeves up to their elbows. They sat around the table, talking genially about their work and their neighbors.

When George's mother placed a custard pie on the table, his father remembered their weekly custom. "Our meal's almost finished, so time to share your news. Benjamin, let's start with you today."

Dr. Connor accepted the slice of pie George's mother offered him. "Spring brings insects. I was called out to one farm for a child's rash that turned out to be flea and mosquito bites."

Hildy made a face. "Ugh! Poor child must have been miserable."

"Who was it?" George's father asked. "Did you tell them about diatomaceous soil?"

"Diato- what?" Abigail asked.

"It's a special kind of soil made from mineral deposits," Simon Mason explained. "It was originally used to make dynamite, and it kills all kinds of bugs. You can buy it at the hardware store."

"First of all," Dr. Connor replied, "I can't tell you who it was, and, yes, I did tell the mother about ways to kill the insects. I'll go back this week and make sure the little boy is better."

Hildy shuddered. "Sounds dreadful."

Simon gestured to Hildy. "Why don't you go next? What's your news?"

"According to the owner of Mason Construction," Hildy said with a nod of her head toward George, "the first house is almost finished. Andrew and I plan to tour it on Friday."

"Well, well," Helen said. "This calls for a celebration."

"Not yet," George responded. "I expect the next house to go quicker, but no celebrations until all ten are done."

"George got a sign for the business," Greta volunteered. "It's beautiful."

"Yeah," George scoffed, "but it almost flattened poor Greta."

George's older brother John pointed at him with a fork. "Need some help hanging up a little-bitty sign?"

George refused to take the bait. "Nothing stronger brackets won't fix."

Simon turned to his youngest son. "What's going on at the newspaper, Andrew?"

"I don't want to make my brothers jealous," Andrew said with a saucy grin, "but my editor is sending me to Atlanta. He wants a story about the New York Highlanders' spring training."

"Poor you," John said with feigned pity. "Going to try out for the team while you're there?"

"No, no," Andrew said with a serious expression. "I know they need a good shortstop, but I could never leave you, big brother." The round of groans from his family made Andrew laugh.

As the family's conversation continued, Greta's mind fluctuated between wonder and puzzlement. The Masons were so different from her own family. Helen seemed to relish the accomplishments of her children as they entered the adult world, but Greta's mother had often wished to return to the days when Greta had been a young child. Simon Mason was interested in his children's lives, but Greta's father was a reticent man who spoke to her about business but little else. She'd thought her family loved each other but sitting at the table with the Masons made it clear her family's type of love paled next to George's family.

Simon Mason stood, signaling the end of the meal. Greta remembered how the women split the cleaning chores and decided to help Abigail scrape leftover food off the plates. She stood and reached for a plate, but George stopped her with a touch on the arm.

"Let's go see your kitten."

Greta shook her head and smiled. "I'd like to see them, but I can't take one. My landlady refuses to let me have a pet. Mrs. Walker said, 'If people want to have animals in their houses, they should live in the barn'."

"How rude!" Hildy said and rolled her eyes. "I hope your landlady never visits me. My little dog would be so insulted!"

The other women laughed at Hildy's comment. Greta turned to Abigail. "Do you want to come with us to see the kittens?"

Abigail looked at George before she answered. "Not today. I'll check on them next time I'm here."

Some unspoken communication had passed between George and his sister, but Greta could not decipher the message. George held open the back door, and she stepped through it.

"Oh my!" she gasped. "How beautiful!"

George's eyebrows drew together. "The horse pasture?"

"The wildflowers," she explained. "They weren't here last time."

George shrugged. "I really didn't notice."

Greta moved closer to the wooden fence. "You've got coneflower and cosmos, and see those yellow ones? Those are wild sunflowers. I bet you've got over twenty species in this one pasture."

George leaned against the fence beside her. "Do you want some?"

"Not today. If too many are picked, they won't be able to spread their seeds for next year." Greta kept her gaze on the wildflowers as they walked toward the barn. From a distance, she easily identified bitterweed and violets but couldn't determine if the blue ones were cornflowers or flax. "Wildflowers are wonders to me. No gardener prepares the soil or fertilizes them, but they flourish anyway. They're like little blessings, given to us even though we did nothing to deserve them."

"And there I was," George replied, "ignoring them. Now I'll never see one without thinking of you."

Greta's face warmed. It was the loveliest thing anyone had said to her, and the glow surrounding her heart spread throughout her body.

"Hey look," George said, pointing towards the barn door. "They're waiting for us."

Three gray-and-black striped kittens sat or stood near the entrance, their tails and ears erect. "I can't believe how much they've grown!" Greta exclaimed.

"They're old enough to find new homes now. Mom always takes care of that."

Greta crouched and offered her hand to the kittens. Two of them scampered away, but the light gray kitten leaped into her lap. "Oh! Aren't you the brave one?"

George lowered to one knee. "That cat has definitely chosen you."

"Sorry kitty," Greta cooed to the animal. "The mean old landlady says no. You need to look for someone else." She stood and cuddled the kitten in her arms.

"Let's see the others," George said, leading her deeper into the barn.

Fresh hay had been spread on the floor near the kitten's bed, and Greta settled onto it. "Where's the mother cat?"

"Probably taking a break from her pesky children. That's another sign the babies are ready to leave." George lowered himself until he was sitting next to her.

The light gray kitten sat in Greta's lap. She offered it a piece of hay, and the animal flipped onto its back and batted the stem with its front paws.

George watched her for a few moments. "Greta?"

She continued to play with the kitten. "Hm?"

"I asked you to come today because I wanted a chance to talk to you."

"Something about work?" Her gaze remained on the animal.

"No. I may not have been aware of wildflowers, but I'm very aware of how smoothly everything runs because of you."

The warm feeling ignited by George's earlier comment continued to glow in Greta's chest. When he was near, all her fears and worries evaporated, as if her heart knew where it could mend. "I'm so glad business is going well. I can't wait to see the first house. You said to come on Friday, right?"

"Yeah. I'll ask Andrew to stop by the warehouse and give you a ride to the site. It's too far to walk."

"That will be fine." Greta moved the stalk of hay along the kitten's side, encouraging the animal to search for it.

George watched her in silence as she played with the kitten. What was on his mind? She could continue to wait, or she could spur him to get to the point. Unlike other people she'd trusted, George would never ambush her with cruel remarks. "What did you want to talk to me about?"

George took a deep breath and blew it out. "Before I tell you, I want you to know that no matter what, I hope you keep working with me."

He must need to say something unpleasant. Greta looked at him from the corner of her eyes. "Should I be worried?"

George smiled, looked at the ground, and rubbed the back of his head. "I hope not. The thing is...I'd like to court you."

Everything inside Greta's body came to an abrupt standstill. Her pulse thudded in her ears, deafening her to all other sounds. What had George said? He couldn't be serious. Courting was the precursor to marriage. Did George want to marry her? How could anything so wonderful actually be true?

The ignored kitten sank its tiny teeth into Greta's finger. "Ow!" Greta shook her hand as air rushed into her lungs. She moved the kitten from her lap to the floor and placed a hand over her hurtling heart. George stared at her with intense anxiety, but she could not return his gaze. She must have misheard him. Perhaps her fantasies of love had tricked her into hearing what she'd wanted to hear rather than what he'd actually said.

"Wh-what did you—?" Her voice trembled and her stomach quivered. She breathed deeply and expelled a shaky breath. "C-court me? Like...really court me?"

George seemed to be amused by her reaction. "That's what I said. If you tell me where your father lives, I'll talk to him."

"No!" The idea of George calling on her parents caused her bones to tremble. "I mean, there's no need."

George stretched his long legs in front of him and leaned back on his arms. "Are you at least receptive to the idea, Greta? 'Cause if you don't want me to court you, I'll forget all about it."

Greta covered her face with her hands. Only she could botch a near-proposal from the man of her dreams. Bit-by-bit, reality seeped its way past her muddled mind. He deserved an answer, a thorough, honest answer. "I've never wanted anything more, but I'm not..." She swallowed hard, determined to speak the truth despite the crushing disappointment her confession would cause. "I'm already married, George."

He didn't recoil the way she'd expected. George remained in the same position, apparently unfazed by her revelation. "That's what Benjamin told me. But I'm hoping you'll tell me the whole story. I've never seen your husband, and neither has anyone else in town."

He'd spoken to Dr. Connor? About her?

Dr. Connor knew her story but had apparently kept it secret. She got to her feet and walked slowly toward the barn's wide doorway. George stood and moved to the other side of the entrance, watching her and waiting. The worst of the shock had passed, and wistful reality had taken its place. "It's a long story," Greta said.

George was the embodiment of patience. Leaning against the doorway, his shoulders relaxed and his hands in his pockets, he resembled a heron at water's edge. "I've got all day," he said with a laconic drawl.

"It's a long and humiliating story."

He appeared to be considering her warning. After several long moments, he crossed his arms in front of his chest and faced her. "I can't imagine anything would keep me from wanting you."

If only that were true. No one had wanted Greta. She'd been passed over at school dances, she'd been left on the sidelines at church socials, and her own parents valued her for what she could do rather than for who she was. Greta stepped out of the barn and walked forward a few steps. "Could we take a walk? It would be easier if you weren't staring at me."

George pushed away from the door and grinned. "Sure. There's an orchard on the other side of the stream. Since you like wildflowers, you'll probably like the flowering trees." He extended his hand, silently inviting her to take it.

She shouldn't. Once he knew her story, he'd turn his back on her. She'd continue working in his office, but everything would be altered. He'd look at her differently and undoubtedly regret the words he'd spoken today.

She gazed longingly at his work-hardened hand. If she only had the next hour with him, she was determined to enjoy it. She slipped her hand into his.

"This way," he said, tugging her toward the dirt road in front of the farmhouse.

Greta raised her face to the sun and closed her eyes, content to rely on George to lead her. The sweet smell of the earth and wildflowers comforted her, and she let the burden of impending disappointment drift away on the warm breeze. Harsh reality loomed on the horizon, but, for the next few minutes, she would enjoy the sensation of walking with the man she loved.

The sound of splashing water enticed her to open her eyes. There was a wooden bridge wide enough to accommodate a farm wagon. As they crossed, Greta saw clear water following the contours of the road. A few steps beyond the bridge, they entered a grove of fruit trees crowned in white and pink blossoms.

Greta released George's hand and wove through the trees, her face upturned to the glorious blossoms. Birdsong and the buzz of bees filled the air, and, for just a second, sublime happiness touched her soul. "I've never seen anything so beautiful," Greta gushed. "They do this every spring?"

"Just like clockwork," George answered. "We have apple and cherry trees."

"The smell...oh, that aroma is heavenly." She gripped the slender trunk of a young tree and swung herself around.

"I've never seen anyone enjoy fruit trees as much as you," George said with a laugh.

Suddenly self-conscious, Greta ducked her head and turned her back to him. For a minute, she'd felt as light as a child. But it was time to account for adult mistakes. "Is there a place we can sit?"

"Over there," George answered with a tilt of his head. "Dad keeps empty fruit crates in that shed. I can fashion some kind of bench for us."

Greta heard George rummaging through the shed as she tarried among the trees. When she joined him, he'd arranged the crates into a square, giving her plenty of room to sit.

She eased onto the improvised bench, not sure it would support her weight, and George sat to her right. She looked straight ahead, unwilling to see disappointment on George's face. She was determined to tell the entire story, even though such honesty would reveal the worst things about her. She took a deep breath, let it out, and reached for her courage.

"Do you know where New Canaan is?" she began.

"I've heard of it."

"It's a medium-sized town on the coast. It's bigger than

Brightfield. My father owns the grocery store on Main Street, and we live upstairs.”

“You grew up there?”

Greta nodded. “I went to school with the same group of girls from primary school through high school. Then I watched as each one got married and started having babies. I didn’t have to wonder why I was being passed up. Girls who look like me aren’t chosen.”

“What do you mean? I think you’re beautiful.”

Greta glanced at him over her shoulder. He was sincere— wonderfully, amazingly sincere. “Oh, George. You would be the only one. My own mother describes me as part horse.”

“I know what that’s like,” George said with a resentful tone. “I’ve been called a bear, a bull, and too many other things to remember.”

“But you’re a man. Men are supposed to be big and strong. Women are supposed to be more like Abigail. Or Hildy.”

George scoffed. “Hildy is so thin, she doesn’t even make a shadow.”

Despite the tension of the moment, Greta laughed. Beauty truly must be in the eye of the beholder if George preferred her to Hildy. “I’m glad you think so, but Hildy looks exactly like the idealized models in lady fashion magazines.”

“Well, I wouldn’t know about that.”

“I’ll bring you a copy of *Vogue*. Hildy’s picture is probably on the cover.”

“I’ll pass,” George answered with a sardonic grin.

Greta laughed again. She’d dreaded this moment, but her spirit felt light. “Salesmen called on my father all the time,” she continued. “They took his order and showed him any new products. One of the most frequent was from Washburn Flour Mills in Minneapolis. His name was Emile Franklin.”

“Franklin?”

Greta nodded.

“What was your name before you married?”

“Horvat.”

“Sounds like a good name.”

“Dad says our people came from Croatia, but that was long before me. Anyway, about Emile...he was always friendly, but that’s how salesmen are. Then, a little over a year ago, he started paying special attention to me. When he told me he wanted to get married, I was astounded." Greta laid a hand on her stomach. Sitting beside George on that beautiful spring day didn't upset her, but her stomach seemed to remember how it had churned when Emile had proposed. Her instincts had told her it would be a mistake, but marriage carried the hope of children and family. She'd muted her inner voice and put all her hopes on Emile.

George leaned forward and clasped his hands between his knees. "What did your parents say?"

"They didn't like him. Emile said we would live in Minneapolis, which my mother thought was too far away. I'm an only child, and I suppose she assumed I would live with her forever. My father didn't say much, but he didn't trust Emile."

"Why did you marry him anyway?"

Greta twisted to face him. "Don't you see? He was my only chance. I was well past the age when most girls marry, and my only other option was to be an old maid."

"How old were you?"

"Twenty-eight."

"Hardly old."

Greta shook her head. "You don't understand. It's different for a man. A man can wait until he's in his forties or fifties and then marry a woman in the prime of her childbearing years. But women need to start their families much earlier. I was well on my way to being a childless spinster."

George didn't respond. He rubbed his hands together and gazed at the flowering trees but said nothing. Was he thinking about what she'd just said? Had his feelings for her changed? Greta wished he would say something but knew she must give him time to process her explanation.

Finally, George looked at her. "Did you go to Minneapolis?"

Relief eased Greta's tight stomach. He was still talking to her. "I've never been to Minneapolis. Emile and I got married by a justice of the peace, and then we traveled to Greenville by train. We stayed at the Emerald Hotel for two nights, and then Emile moved us into the boarding house. We lived there for a few months, and Emile would travel a bit, but always come back. Then, one day, he told me he had to go to Washington County. He promised he'd be back in a week."

She'd reached the worst part of her story. George deserved to know what had happened, even though it meant admitting her shame. She stood and walked a few steps away from him. The sun was inching its way to the horizon, turning the sky from bright blue to violet. How had so much time passed? It would be dark by the time they made it back to the farmhouse.

"What happened?" George asked.

Greta turned to face him. "That was the last time I saw Emile Franklin. At first, I was afraid something had happened to him. What if he'd been hurt or killed? I didn't know his family, didn't know anyone to contact, so I sent a letter to Washburn Mills. The company wrote back saying Emile no longer worked for them."

George's dark eyebrows drew together, and his hands fisted on his knees. When he spoke, there was anger in his voice. "He just left you?"

Greta reminded herself George's animosity wasn't directed at her. "It took me a few weeks to arrive at that conclusion, but, yes, he just left me."

George got to his feet and paced back and forth. His elbows were bent, and his fists hovered near his waist, as though ready to hit Emile should her missing husband suddenly appear. Her shadow crossed George's powerful body every time he passed, and she marveled at how different his reaction was to hers. She'd blamed herself, but George was ready to punch Emile. She'd never been one to advocate violence, but knowing George wanted to defend her was a thrilling realization. No one had stood up for her before, but George would. She almost felt sorry for Emile.

After several minutes of striding in front of the benches, George visibly cooled. His shoulders dropped and he blew out a breath. "It makes me so angry to think about him hurting you that way."

Greta wanted to throw her arms around him, but embracing George was out of the question. She folded her arms in front of stomach and continued her story. "After I realized Emile wasn't coming back, I thought about going home but…" Greta turned her back to George.

She didn't hear his footsteps on the soft grass, but she felt his warm hand on her shoulder. "Why didn't you?" he asked.

"Our families are very different. I've seen how your family interacts with each other. For all the teasing, it's obvious there's a lot of love. If Dr. Connor left Abigail, your mother would welcome her back, and your brothers would make sure Dr. Connor paid for hurting their sister."

"He'd pay with his face," George said in a menacing voice.

Greta was sure Dr. Connor could hold his own in a fistfight, but she was glad he'd never come to blows with George. "Not to worry," she reassured him. "Dr. Connor is one of the best men I know."

George removed his hand from her shoulder. "I take it your family isn't the same?"

Greta shrugged. How could she tell the truth without disparaging her parents? "If I'd gone home and explained that Emile had abandoned me, I would have been shamed. My mother would say I should have never left, that my duty is to take care of her when she grows old, that any man who'd want to marry me must have ulterior motives...the list is endless."

George's eyebrows shot up, and his jaw slackened. "You've never told them?"

"I write them every week. I tell them about my interesting work, and I never mention Emile. Not one word."

George's expression showed his disbelief. "Why haven't you sought a divorce?"

"Because there hasn't been a reason. Even if I wanted a divorce, I have no idea how to find Emile."

"I plan on giving you a reason."

Greta's eyes stung with unshed tears. How could he still want her? What had she ever done to deserve the esteem of this good man? She'd grown accustomed to one-sided love, relationships that only existed in her fantasies, but George was real. He was solid muscle and durable bone and as real as the ground beneath her feet. She'd told him everything, and he still wanted to court her. How had she earned such a miracle?

George straddled the bench so that he faced her. She had one more thing to say, so she called on her last ounce of courage. "This seems to be the moment for confessions, so I'm going to take a deep breath and admit something else I've been keeping secret."

"I'm listening."

"I'm falling in love with you, George Mason. I've told myself it's impossible, I've chided myself for being a romantic fool, and I've—"

George's lips stopped Greta from confessing more. Greta leaned into him, wrapping her arms around his neck and giving herself to him. His kiss was as strong as the rest of him. His arms went around her back, pulling her closer, and his lips claimed hers.

Greta's heart beat fast, pleading for more, searching for the love George offered. How could this be genuine? After all her mistakes, after the years of being passed over, how had she found the one man who truly wanted her?

George ended the kiss and pressed his forehead against hers. His breathing was ragged, and his lips glistened with her moisture. On his neck, a vein bulged with his uneven pulse. She placed one finger on the vein and felt his body's throbbing rhythm. George took her hand away from his neck and nestled her head on his shoulder.

"The things you've been through, Greta. The only explanation for such malice is selfishness. Your mother thought only of herself, not what was best for you. And the man you married...he never intended to be a real husband. He took advantage of your situation for his own pleasure."

"I let him."

"How could you have known? You took him at his word, not realizing there was no integrity behind it."

Greta pushed away from the comfort of George's chest and took a deep breath. "As you can see, I'm stuck in the bed I made. I can't get a divorce. And as much as I'd like to be courted by you, I am not free. I can be your bookkeeper but nothing more."

A slow smile spread across George's face. "Greta, if you think I'd give up that easily, you definitely don't know me."

CHAPTER SIX

Tearing down one house and building another had taken much longer than George had expected, but one new home was finally ready. As he stood near the worktable he'd fashioned from plywood and sawhorses, he surveyed the bungalow. Four tapered columns set on plinths supported an overhanging eave that covered an ample front porch, and a wide gable dormer took up the center of the second floor. Inside, there were four bedrooms and a modern kitchen. As specified, George had included gas lines for heating and cooking, electricity, and plumbing tied into the city's water department. He'd hired ladies from the neighborhood to clean the construction mess his workers had left inside, but, thanks to two days of rain, the painters were just now finishing the outside.

Henry waded through one of the deep puddles surrounding the house and approached George. "I'll find some boards to make a bridge our guests can walk on. Not everyone's goin' to have a pair of these new rubber boots to keep their feet dry." He raised his foot to show off the muddy black boot.

"How'd the cleaning ladies get in?" George asked.

"Don't know. I guess they jumped. Or flew."

"Well," George replied, "I'm not sure Hildy can fly, so you'd better make that bridge for her. She'll be here soon."

Three women carrying mops, buckets, and towels appeared on the front porch. "Just a minute!" Henry called. He went to the pile of scrap lumber, selected two wide planks, and carried them to the large puddle that fronted the porch. After positioning them across the narrowest part, he motioned for the women to proceed. They crossed easily, but the planks sank a few inches when the third woman walked across. They gathered near George's worktable.

"Mr. Mitchell," said a gaunt woman in a faded green dress, "we've been wonderin' which family gets to move into this new house."

Henry rubbed his cheek. "I've been thinkin' on that. Seems to me the fair thing to do is let whoever's lived here the longest be the first to move. How does that sit with you?"

The women looked at each other. "I guess that's fair," the same woman answered. "But the Dowling family has been here the longest, and they've only got two children. Seems like a waste of a big house for just four people."

Henry slid his hands into the back pockets of his work pants. "Well, what do you suggest? All the houses goin' to have three or four bedrooms."

The women looked at each other again before a gray-haired woman wearing a blue apron spoke. "If you're goin' to follow the rule of longest residents get first pick, can we make you a list? If the Dowlings don't want to move into this big house, then the next family on the list could have a chance."

"I'm for whatever you ladies think is fair," Henry answered. "Last thing I want to do is cause bad feelin's."

The woman in the green dress spoke again. "We'll let you know. Thanks for listenin'."

The residents walked cautiously around the numerous puddles toward the line of remaining shacks. Henry sagged against the worktable and glanced at George. "I'm not so sure how my new job's goin' to work out."

"When Hildy asked you to act as property manager, didn't you know diplomat was part of the job?" George asked.

Henry shook his head. "Not really. Seems like I'm to be a combination fix-it man, rent collector, and all 'round problem solver."

"Why did you agree to take it on?"

Henry rubbed his whiskered cheek. "Well, it seemed like a good opportunity. You won't need me after this project, and I like to keep busy."

"Who says I won't need you? I'm already scouting for more business. You can work with me as long as you'd like."

Henry looked at the ground and smiled. "George, when you asked me to help out on this project, it was like the answer to a prayer. Sittin' around doin' nothin' was 'bout to make me crazier than a dog with a feather tied to its tail." Before George could respond, Henry lifted his chin toward the line of shacks. "Hildy's comin'."

The red Oldsmobile Limited driving down the dirt road was unmistakable. Few people in Brightfield could afford such a luxury vehicle. The automobile's tires splashed through several puddles, muddying the pristine red finish, and stopped a few feet from George. His brother, Andrew, hopped out of the driver's seat.

"Hey there, big brother. Can't wait to see what you've been up to." Andrew jogged around the car to open the passenger door. Hildy slid out of the front seat and turned to help Greta climb out of the rear.

Remembering what Greta had told him about Hildy, George took a few moments to compare the two. Hildy was shorter and thinner. The black trim on her pale pink dress outlined her gentle curves and a wide-brimmed hat gave her a top-heavy appearance. He knew enough about construction to recognize the strategy behind the design. His eye was drawn to the black trim rather than Hildy's angular figure, and the mound of pink flowers atop her large hat made her seem taller.

Greta's brown business suit did little to flatter her full-bodied figure, and her brown hat resembled an overturned bucket. With her colorful dress and hat, Hildy reminded him of a spring flower. Greta, however, matched the muddy road. He understood Greta's point about Hildy's style, but he still preferred Greta. Andrew had been drawn to Hildy, but George had only thought of her as a client. He'd done various jobs for her in the past, and she'd certainly boosted his dream of owning his own business, but romance had never crossed his mind.

Hildy extended her gloved hand as she approached. "The house is beautiful, George! So much better than I imagined!"

George took her hand in his, careful not to squeeze too hard. "Glad you like it. The painters will be finished in a few hours."

"I can't wait to see inside." Hildy turned to Andrew. "Remember what was here before? Can you believe the difference?"

"Like night and day," Andrew agreed. "I wouldn't mind living here myself."

Hildy slipped her arm through Andrew's. "Let's walk around the back."

While Hildy and Andrew made their way around the standing water, George walked toward Greta. She welcomed him with a broad smile, and, since no one was nearby, he gathered her into his arms. This was the woman he wanted. Her powerfully built body overflowed with health and strength. A woman like Greta could withstand the storms of life. She could bear children, raise them with love, and protect them when necessary. She was his match in every way.

"That's one beautiful house," Greta said.

"I'll build you one. Whenever and wherever you want." He felt laughter pass through her body. "Or would you prefer a bigger one?"

She stepped back and looked into his face. "No one ever offered to build me a house before."

"If we were alone, I'd kiss you."

Greta rose to her tiptoes and kissed his cheek. "Will that hold you?"

"If it has to."

Greta's smile was one part girlish and one part temptress.

George yearned to make her his. He wanted her in his mornings and his nights. He wanted her present and her future. There had to be a way to free her from the past.

The nearby sound of voices convinced him to release her. "George!" Andrew called. "Come show us the inside!"

George led Greta toward the newly constructed house. Henry stood on the porch, rubbing his hands together like an eager child. "We got it all cleaned up. Walk across that wooden plank at the end of the puddle."

Andrew scowled at the wide pool of water that stretched from one end of the porch to the other. "This is no puddle, Mr. Mitchell. I believe you've built a moat."

Hildy lifted her skirt in preparation to cross but seemed confused by Henry's instructions. "I don't see the plank."

Henry walked to the end of the porch and peered at the water. "The darned thing sank into the mud. Hold on. I'll fix it."

Andrew squinted into the water. "I see it." Without saying another word, Andrew scooped his wife into his arms.

"Oh!" Hildy yelped in surprise. "Andrew!"

"A few inches of water won't hurt my boots. Besides, I haven't carried you like this since I carried you over the threshold."

The painters stopped working to watch. Hildy laughed and wrapped one arm around Andrew's neck. He crossed the board easily, carried his wife to the center of the porch, and gently deposited her on the top step. The painters applauded Andrew's display of gallantry which he acknowledged with a tip of his hat. Hildy's smile beamed love as she kissed him on the cheek.

On the far side of the puddle, George watched his brother with interest. He'd been surprised when Andrew had announced his marriage to Hildy, but he had to admit his little brother had grown into a man of merit. Although he'd wed the richest woman in town, Hildy's fortune had nothing to do with the love Andrew showed for her.

Hildy and Andrew walked toward the front door, but before they entered, Hildy turned back to speak to Greta. "Aren't you coming?"

Greta waved at Hildy. "If I can find a canoe, I'll row across the moat and join you."

Hildy spoke to Henry. George couldn't hear their conversation, but imagined she was asking Henry to replace the plank bridge for Greta. However, there was no way George would let his little brother show him up.

"Your turn," he said to Greta, placing one arm across her back and the other behind her thighs.

Greta jerked away. "What? No. You don't have to try...I'll wait for the board or...I'll go through the back door."

Why did she resist? "There aren't any steps at the back door yet, and I'm not going to let your shoes get wet."

Greta covered her reddening cheeks with her ungloved hands and dropped her voice to a near whisper. "I'm too heavy, George. You'll drop me."

"Don't be ridiculous." He had no idea how much she weighed, but George knew his strength. Without giving her a chance to protest, he lifted her into his arms.

Greta yelped in surprise and looked at George with wide eyes. "You picked me up so easily."

"Of course. Now hold tight while I carry you across."

Greta's mouth dropped and her eyebrows shot up as George effortlessly walked across the submerged plank. At the top step, he gingerly lowered her until her feet touched the ground.

"No one has ever done that before," she said with breathless incredulity.

George shrugged one shoulder. "I can't speak for other men, but to me, you don't weigh more than a box of feathers."

Laughter danced in Greta's eyes as she threw her arms around his neck. "I think I just fell in love with you."

Before George could react, Hildy joined Greta on the step. Was it his imagination, or did that glint in Hildy's eye mean she'd guessed his feelings for Greta?

Hildy simply smiled and took Greta's arm. "Now George, show me what you've done inside this beautiful house."

Hildy and Greta wandered from room to room, commenting appreciatively about the built-in bookcases and flawless wood paneling. "George, that kitchen is a marvel," Hildy gushed. "Everything is shiny and modern. A kitchen like that would even entice me to cook."

Greta moved to stand at his side. "It's amazing. The house isn't that big, but there's ample storage. I love the reading nook in the main room."

George reached for her hand and led her through the front door and onto the wide porch. Once they were alone, he pulled her into his arms. "I'm glad you like it."

She rested her head on his shoulder. "It's perfect for a family."

George tightened his hold. "Someday, I want to sit on a porch like this and hold you for hours and hours. Just being with you calms me. Makes me believe everything will be all right."

She snuggled closer and sighed. "I feel the same way when I'm with you."

George kissed the top of her head. He wasn't sure how, but he was going to make that wish come true.

***

As she rode back to the boarding house in Hildy's car, Greta couldn't stop smiling. The afternoon had started like any other, but George had changed her day from ordinary to remarkable. When he looked at her, he didn't see a woman who was too tall, too big, and too muscular. George thought her attractive. He wanted to kiss her and embrace her, not use her as a cook and housekeeper. He wanted to court her.

She'd had a week to think about the things he'd said in the orchard, but because of the push to finish the first house, she'd seen very little of him. Of course she wanted him to court her, but she'd ruined her chance by marrying a scoundrel. However, the painful reality of her situation couldn't constrain her joy. George wanted her. In him, she'd found approval and appreciation, affection and desire. Emile had used her to satisfy his lust, but George wanted more than that. George loved her spirit and her body. How could she not embrace a promise like that?

Andrew parked the automobile in front of Greta's boarding house. He slid from behind the wheel and offered his hand to help her climb out of the back seat. "Thank you for the ride," she said.

"Anytime," he answered with a charming smile. "Will I see you at lunch on Sunday?"

Of course she wanted to join the Masons again, but she hadn't been invited. "I'm not sure."

Hildy leaned across the front seat and looked at her through the open door. "I hope you'll come."

Greta returned Hildy's smile. It was getting harder and harder to dislike Hildy. For all her perfection, she was also friendly, generous, and kindhearted. "Thanks. I'll see you at church."

"I'll walk you to the door," Andrew offered.

"Don't bother," Greta said. "It's only a few feet."

Andrew stood by the motorcar and watched as Greta walked to the entrance. She waved before entering the house and then closed the door behind her.

Mrs. Walker, her middle-aged, plump landlady, hurried toward her. "Mrs. Franklin," she began, adjusting her wire-rimmed spectacles, "you have a visitor."

Greta's heart skipped a beat. Were her parents here? They were the only ones outside of Brightfield who knew where she lived. "A visitor?"

"Yes," Mrs. Walker answered breathlessly. "She's waiting for you in the front room."

Greta removed her hat and set it and her purse on the hall table. A tiny woman sat on the chintz-covered sofa in the parlor, drowning amid the deep upholstery. Wearing a dark blue dress with a matching cloche hat, the woman stared at Greta with wide, dark eyes. Greta turned to look at Mrs. Walker in a silent attempt to confirm this unknown woman was looking for her. The landlady nodded, smiled, and walked away from the door.

Relieved her mother hadn't paid an unexpected visit, Greta stepped toward the stranger. "I'm Greta Franklin. Are you looking for me?"

The woman jumped to her feet. "Oh yes. My name is Millie Franklin. I'm from Edina, Minnesota. Do you know where that is?"

Franklin? Greta's stomach tightened. Was this woman one of Emile's relatives? She was too young to be his mother, but she could easily be a sister. "No. I don't know that part of the country very well. Won't you sit down?"

Millie clutched a small purse in her gloved hands and resumed her seat. She was visibly nervous, and Greta's wariness shot higher. "What can I do for you?" Greta asked.

"I'm looking for Emile Franklin. I got a copy of his sales route from Washburn Mills, and I've been following it, hoping I'd run into him. When I got to New Canaan, the grocer there ... a Mr. Horvat?"

She looked at Greta for confirmation. Greta nodded. The grocer, of course, was her father.

"Anyway," Millie continued, "Mr. Horvat told me Emile had married his daughter and that she lived here in Brightfield. He gave me this address. Are you Emile's wife?"

Who was this mouse of a woman? Her words shot out of her mouth in rapid succession and her gaze darted around the room while she spoke. "Mr. Horvat is my father. Emile and I were married last year."

Millie covered her face with her hands and doubled over. Was she crying? No sound came from her small body, but her shoulders shuddered as though wracked by sobs. Greta placed a tentative hand on Millie's back.

She could feel Millie's backbone through the thin dress fabric. The poor woman trembled with each breath, and Greta braced herself for the next thing Millie would say. If news of Emile's marriage had impacted her so fiercely, whatever followed couldn't be good.

After several long moments, Millie took several deep breaths, straightened her back, and whisked away her tears with her gloved fingers. "I need to tell you something very shocking. You seem like a nice lady, and I'm sorry to have to tell you this, but I married Emile two years ago."

CHAPTER SEVEN

No. It wasn't possible. Millie was simply mistaken. Maybe there were two men with the name Emile Franklin. An invisible shield formed over Greta's heart as she fought against believing Millie's outlandish claim.

Greta sprang to her feet. "You're wrong, Mrs. Franklin. I'm sorry you've come so far to find me, but it simply can't be true."

Millie looked at Greta with pity, but her sympathy did nothing to pacify the anger building inside of Greta. "I know how you feel," Millie said in a soft voice. "I felt the same way when your father told me you'd married Emile."

"Maybe you've got the wrong person," Greta argued. "There could easily be another Emile Franklin."

Millie stood and placed her hands on Greta's stiff arms. "Edina is close to Minneapolis. That's where I met Emile. He was just beginning to work for Washburn Mills then. We had a little wedding in my church, and, just before our first anniversary, we had a little boy. His name is Joseph Anthony Franklin."

"You have a child?"

"Oh, he's a wonderful little boy. Even though Emile left us, I'm very happy to have Joey."

The weight of the truth threatened to bring Greta to her knees. She sagged against the wall as the impact of Emile's actions became clear. He'd married Millie in front of a minister, but for Greta, he'd gone to a justice of the peace. He had a son. Emile had abandoned a child!

Millie led her to the sofa, and Greta sank into the soft cushions. She wouldn't cry. Not until she was in her room alone. Emile had taken advantage of Greta, but Millie had been treated much worse.

Greta swallowed, pushed down her mounting anger, and faced Emile's other wife. "Emile told me he was going to Washington County to call on a customer, but I never heard from him again."

Millie nodded, apparently not surprised by Greta's story. She opened her small purse and withdrew a folded piece of white paper. "This is Emile's sales route. After Brightfield, he goes to Fort Madison, then New Wexford and West Markham." She turned the paper over. "The mill gave me this address. This is where they sent his final check."

The address was in New Wexford, just across the state line. Perhaps Emile had settled there. "Are you going to keep looking for him?" Greta asked.

"I have to," Millie answered. "I've been living with my parents, but that isn't working out. My father never misses a chance to tell me how foolish I was, and my mother treats me like I'm too stupid to care for my child. I want to leave Edina and move someplace where no one knows me. I've always dreamed of being one of those working women who have fascinating careers. Joey's going to grow up and leave me one day, and I want a life of my own when he does. I need Emile to give me money so I can make a fresh start."

Greta certainly sympathized with Millie's situation, but how would tiny Millie stand up to Emile? He could be domineering, and he resented people who disagreed with him. "How are you….I mean, what if he refuses?"

A sly smile crossed Millie's lips. "I have a father and two brothers. If I locate him, they'll come and...uh….*convince* him."

Poor Emile. Not that he shouldn't support his child, but the image of Emile trying to stand up to Millie's family made Greta wince. George had described what he and his brothers would do if Dr. Connor mistreated Abigail. Millie's brothers were apparently no different.

"Do you want to come with me?" Millie asked.

Greta blinked at the little woman. If Millie was Emile's lawful wife, where did that leave her? Or was Greta's marriage legal and Millie's wasn't? Millie's may have preceded hers, but if Emile was a bigamist, there was no telling what other fraudulent schemes he'd committed.

The possibilities and depth of Emile's deceit buzzed through Greta's mind like flies over carrion. What else had he done? Who else had he hurt?

She needed to talk to George. He'd be able to sort things out.

Greta got to her feet, retrieved her purse and hat, and walked toward the front door.

"Where are you going?" Millie asked.

Through the window, Greta could see it was dark. George wouldn't be at the work site, but he might be at the warehouse. She turned to Millie. "Excuse me. I need to make a telephone call."

But Mrs. Walker had no telephone in her boarding house. The clinic had one, and Greta could go there, but Dr. Connor and Abigail were most likely eating dinner. She should wait until the next day. She'd call George in the morning or see him tomorrow afternoon. Despite the near panic floating through her body, there really wasn't any reason to rush. Nothing would change between tonight and tomorrow morning.

Greta took a deep breath and let it out slowly. Then she did it again. It was a technique Dr. Connor had suggested when she'd consulted him about the ceaseless headaches that had plagued her last summer. Not only had it eased her pain, she'd also learned decisions made in the midst of agitation were never helpful. She turned slowly and faced Millie. "Do you have a place to stay tonight?"

Millie nodded. "Your landlady took my bag and told me she has a small room if I need it, but I wanted to talk to you before I accepted. I know I've upset you, and you're probably anxious for me to leave."

"You're only the messenger," Greta said with a reassuring smile. "Emile hurt both of us, and I certainly understand the need to find him. Do you plan to take the train to Fort Madison?"

"Yes," Millie answered. "It doesn't leave until three o'clock tomorrow, so I have plenty of time."

Greta returned her hat and purse to the hallway table. "Stay the night if you'd like. I need to talk to my employers tomorrow morning, and then I'll be able to decide about going with you. Is that all right?"

Millie moved to stand in front of Greta. "Of course. I didn't know how you would react when I told you about me and Emile, so I thank you for taking it so well."

"I appreciate your kind words," Greta replied, "but I'm not sure I deserve them. Now, let me show you where the dining room is. Dinner must be ready by now."

***

Greta was dressed before dawn the next morning. The low rays of sunlight made her shadow stretch to monstrous proportions as she hurried along the sidewalk toward the clinic. Dr. Connor's first patient was scheduled for eight o'clock. At this early hour, he would either be preparing for the day or eating breakfast. Greta decided to try the back door to the living quarters before using her key to open the clinic's front door.

Abigail responded to Greta's quiet tap. "Greta! I almost didn't hear you. Is something wrong?"

"No," Greta said as she entered the kitchen. "I need to speak to Dr. Connor about missing the next few days of work."

Dr. Connor had been sitting in his usual seat at the table, but he stood before speaking to Greta. "Are you feeling ill?"

"No, it's nothing like that," Greta hastened to clarify.

"Sit down," Abigail said, "and have a cup of coffee. Have you eaten breakfast?"

Greta took the chair across from Dr. Connor, and when she'd been seated, he sat down as well. Abigail placed a cup of black coffee in front of her and then returned to the stove.

Dr. Connor had patients' charts on the table in front of him. He closed the top folder and gave Greta his full attention.

"I had a visitor at Mrs. Walker's boarding house last night. It seems my husband has another wife."

Dr. Connor's eyebrows shot up. "You met her?"

Greta told him about Millie's visit. Abigail set a plate of food in front of Benjamin, but neither one of them interrupted her account. When she finished, Abigail was the first to respond.

"I think you must go. Tell me what's coming up for this week, and I'll take care of whatever I can."

The frown on Dr. Connor's face expressed his concern. "We'll manage fine, but I'm worried about confronting this man. What do you hope to accomplish?"

"I need to find out if I'm truly married or not," Greta said.

"Surely, he'll at least tell me that much."

"Have you told George?" Abigail asked.

Greta sipped her coffee before answering. Abigail must know about George's desire to court her. Why else would she ask such a question? "Not yet. The train doesn't leave until three. That should give me plenty of time to get this week's payroll ready. Everything else can wait."

Abigail shook her head. "I'm not concerned about George's business. He'll want to know about your plan to search for your husband. Call him now."

Greta drained her cup and stood. "Thanks. All right if I go through the connecting door?"

"Of course," Abigail answered. "You don't have to ask."

Greta left the kitchen, walked through the parlor, and passed through the open door that led to the clinic hallway. Her heart beat faster in anticipation of speaking to George. Her news would surprise him, but there was a possibility she was free to marry. Unless she'd misjudged him, he'd be happy to learn that piece of information.

Greta picked up the candlestick phone on her desk and asked the town operator to connect her to the Mason farmhouse. Helen's tinny voice answered. "Hello."

"Helen, this is Greta. How are you this morning?"

"Fine, thank you. Are you calling from the clinic? Is everything all right?"

"There's nothing to worry about. I was hoping to catch George before he went to the building site this morning."

"Oh, I'm sorry but, he's already left. I think he's going to the warehouse first. He said he had to load materials so he could start the next house."

"Thank you," Greta said. "I'll telephone him there."

"Wait, Greta," Helen said hurriedly. "Will you ask Abigail if she's free to talk?"

Greta didn't want even a second to delay her from telephoning George, and who knew how long Helen would talk to her daughter? "Is it all right if I ask Abigail to telephone you after I speak to George? I'm afraid he'll leave the warehouse before I talk to him."

"Oh, of course. I didn't think of that. Fine, Greta. I'll see you soon."

Gratitude filled Greta's heart. Helen had understood without Greta explaining the whole thing. "Thanks, Helen."

She rang for the operator again. This time Henry Mitchell answered the call with his usual gravelly voice. "Mason Construction."

"Good morning, Mr. Mitchell. This is Greta calling."

Henry's voice had a smile. "Hello there! What are you doin' this fine spring morning?"

"I'm trying to get in touch with George before he goes to the work site. Is he there?"

"He is, but he's outside right now. Want him to call you back?"

It would be easier if she could tell him in person but walking to the warehouse would take at least half an hour. "How long will he be there?"

"Hard to say. We're loading lumber right now, and once the wagon's full, we'll head out."

"Will you ask if he can wait until I get there?"

"Sure! Anythin' for you!"

Greta smiled at the way Henry treated her with unwavering kindness. The workers described him as grouchy and cantankerous, but he turned on the charm for her. "I appreciate it. I'll be there as soon as I can."

She replaced the earpiece of the telephone into its cradle and returned to the kitchen. Abigail sat at the table alone. "Did you find George?"

"He's at the warehouse. I'll walk over there now." Greta picked up her purse and headed for the back door.

"That will take too long," Abigail protested. "Let me drive you."

Greta's steps came to an abrupt stop. She'd never heard of Abigail driving before. "I didn't know you could drive."

"Andrew's been teaching me. I may not be as good a driver as Benjamin, but I can get us to George's warehouse."

It would be much faster, and George wouldn't have to delay getting to the work site, but an inexperienced driver usually landed upside-down in a ditch. "If you're sure."

Abigail jumped to her feet. "I can tell you're reluctant to ride with me, but I'll get you there in one piece. Then I'll come back and do my best to help Benjamin. Give me a few seconds to grab my hat, and we'll be off." She hurried toward the bedroom.

"Oh!" Greta called after her, "Before I forget, your mother wants to talk to you."

"I'll call her when I get back," Abigail said when she returned to the kitchen. "Now hop in Benjamin's motorcar, and I'll drive as fast as possible with my eyes closed until we get to the warehouse."

Greta's eyebrows shot up.

"Just kidding," Abigail said as she hurried through the back door.

CHAPTER EIGHT

George sat in the warehouse office and listened intently as Greta explained why she needed to miss work. His emotions swung wildly between outrage, concern, and hope. He knew her so-called husband was a thoughtless lowlife who hadn't cared about anything except himself, but George had never considered her marriage might not be valid.

He struggled to keep calm. The last thing he wanted was to upset Greta more than she already was. "Why do you want to go with this woman? What did you say her name was?"

"Millie. Millie Franklin. She and Emile have a son, and she hopes to get money from him."

Thoughts of Greta's husband ignited a slow burn in George's stomach. "You know, I already detested your husband, but abandoning a child….that's the worst part of all this."

Greta propped her elbow on the desk and rested her head in her hand. "I agree. I've always hoped to have a family someday, but I'm relieved to not have a reason to be tied to Emile."

George pushed away mental pictures of Greta with another man. He planned to claim her as his mate. That's all that really mattered. "What do you hope will happen when you find him?"

Greta reached across the desk and used both of her hands to hold George's. "This is where my feelings get all mixed up. I regret marrying him, and sometimes I berate myself for going through with it, but I remind myself I never suspected he would abandon me. I was determined to make the best of it. Now, however….well, now I hope the marriage wasn't legal. Because if it wasn't, I'll be free of Emile and free to love you."

How strange that something good could come from her husband's dishonesty. Perhaps he wouldn't have to wait for legal proceedings and could wed Greta before the end of spring. "I don't see how your marriage could be legal. He either married this other woman first, or he married someone before her. How could hers be a sham and yours be genuine?"

"That's just one answer I need from him."

"What else?"

"Whether or not he'll divorce me."

If Greta was lawfully married to the louse, he'd agree to a divorce. George would make sure of it. "I don't think you need his consent. He abandoned you. Surely that's sufficient reason to grant a woman a divorce."

"I suppose it would be easier if my wedding was a sham. That way, no divorce would be necessary. Either way, I should probably speak to a lawyer just to make sure. Know any good ones?"

"No, but Hildy will. She had a lawyer in Greenville draw up our contract."

George moved his chair and sat beside Greta so he could wrap his arms around her. They sat in silence, taking and giving comfort, calming doubts about their future, and simply resting in each other's soothing embrace. After several long minutes, George kissed her head. "How would you feel about me going with you?"

Greta put a few inches between them so she could look up at his face. "How can you? You're about to start the second and third houses."

"Henry can handle it. I don't like to put too much on him, but he'll be fine for a few days."

Greta leaned against George's side and gazed into space. He resolved to be patient, to give her all the thinking time she needed, but restraining his natural desire to do something — to do anything — was more difficult than he thought. If he met Emile, his first instinct would be to punch him in the face. All things considered, such an action would probably not help Greta.

Greta shifted slightly in her chair and looked at him. "I know you want to protect me, but Emile has never harmed me. Not physically that is. And this is my dragon to slay. After I confront him, I want to come back and rest in your arms. When you embrace me, I feel as though nothing can touch me. Cruel words and rejections and harsh criticisms have no power when you're at my side."

She'd just asked him to do nothing. To wait at home while she went to war. There was something fundamentally wrong about that arrangement, but he had faith in her. If any woman could slay a dragon, it would be Greta. His mother had taught him women had tough spirits and tender hearts. He could see that in Greta. Her so-called husband had hurt her, but he hadn't destroyed her. She had inner toughness that would enable her to stand up to him, and she had the tenderness to open her heart to George.

He lowered his head and kissed her perfectly sculpted lips. "Will you send a telegram to let me know when you'll be back? I know they charge by the word, but could you add a short message to let me know if your news is good or bad?"

Greta returned his kiss. "I'm coming back to you. Whether I'm married or unmarried, single or divorced, I'm coming back."

He pulled her close and kissed her. "See that you do," he whispered. Otherwise, he'd be searching for her.

***

By two o'clock, Greta had completed the week's payroll for Mason Construction, met with Abigail to explain the tasks she'd need to complete, and packed the things she'd need for the trip. She and Millie set off for the train station, their purses in one hand and their traveling bags in the other.

Millie seemed excited to be leaving. "You're so lucky to have found such a nice boarding house. The room I had last night is nicer than the one I have at home. And the food is so good. Why, I ate so much at breakfast, I thought I'd never have room for lunch, but wouldn't you know I cleaned my plate. Another good thing is how close the boarding house is to the station. Of course, Brightfield doesn't seem to be a very large place. Probably everything is close."

Millie hadn't been so talkative the night before. She'd been nervous when she'd delivered her news, but now that she was relaxed, the spigot had been opened.

At the station, Greta bought one ticket for Fort Madison, then stepped aside so Millie could do the same. Luckily, she found a passenger car with plenty of empty seats, and she and the other Mrs. Franklin were soon on their way.

During the two-hour journey, Millie talked incessantly about her family and her son, but, as the train pulled into the Fort Madison station, Millie's conversation slowed to a halt.

She must be nervous, Greta realized. Just like Friday night, Millie's uncertainty consumed her words.

Millie withdrew the folded piece of paper from her handbag and showed it to Greta. "Emile called on two merchants here. I have an address for Thompson Grocery and another for Cagle's Emporium. Do you want to go together, or should we split up?"

What have you done at the other stores? Just asked for Emile?"

76

"That's right. I tell them I'm trying to find Emile Franklin and ask if he's called on them."

"Do you tell them you're his wife?"

Millie shifted her gaze from Greta to the window. "I did at first, but then I realized some of the men were trying to protect Emile from me. Now I say I'm his sister, and our parents are trying to get in touch with him. That works better."

Greta didn't look forward to lying, but she needed to find Emile. Pretending to be his sister wouldn't hurt anyone. "We might as well go separately. The next stop on this line is New Wexford, and it leaves at seven fifteen."

Millie shifted in her seat and returned the folded paper to her purse. "I think we should try to make it. That way we won't have to pay for a hotel here."

Although her ears were tired from Millie's incessant talk, Greta found herself warming up to this sparrow of a woman. Millie was practical and straightforward, two qualities Greta had always valued. "Any preference about which store to visit?"

"No," answered Millie. "I'm going to ask the station clerk for directions and if he'll watch our bags for a few hours."

Greta stood, retrieved her traveling bag, and followed Millie inside the brick building that housed the railway offices. She towered over the petite woman, a position that usually made her feel ungainly and awkward, but fewer self-recriminations sprang into her mind this time. She needn't look like someone else to be beautiful. She was unique. Some men preferred small women like Millie. George liked women her size. He understood how unsettling it could be to stand out in a crowd, but he'd recognized her as his match. For the first time in her life, Greta wouldn't have traded places with any other woman.

A few minutes later, she and Millie parted ways. Cagle's Emporium was the farthest, and Greta volunteered to visit that establishment since her long legs could cover the distance faster. Following the clerk's instructions, she sprinted across the congested street and headed toward the clock tower of City Hall. Striding down the sidewalk, she mentally rehearsed what she would say to the grocer. She should probably prepare for her encounter with Emile, but there was no guarantee she and Millie would find him in Fort Madison. Besides, she was certain her anger would inspire the necessary words.

As the ticket agent had told her, Cagle's Emporium was directly across the town square from City Hall. The owner had painted the ornate facade gold and white, but the dusty windows showed everyday items like cleaning supplies and canned vegetables. Her father would have said it was a case of too much promise and too little delivery.

A small bell attached to the door rang cheerily as Greta entered. An adolescent boy wearing a full apron greeted her from behind the counter. "Good afternoon, ma'am. How may I help you?"

She knew firsthand how difficult it could be to wait on the public, so she smiled broadly and approached the clerk. "Good afternoon. I'm hoping to speak to the manager of your store. Is he available?"

Traces of panic edged the boy's eyes. "Is there a problem?"

"No," Greta hurried to explain. "I want to talk to the manager about a salesman who calls here. Nothing's wrong."

The boy's shoulders dropped as relief eased his worry. "Yes, ma'am. I'll call the manager." He ducked through a doorway to what Greta assumed was the storeroom.

Greta had expected the manager to be similar to her father, but the person who entered was an attractive middle-aged woman wearing a stylish gold dress. Her blonde hair was piled atop her head in an intricate coiffure, and her lips and cheeks had been tinted with rouge. "I am Mrs. Patterson, the manager," she said in a cultured voice. "How may I help you?"

Greta took a breath, remembered the fiction Millie had created, and smiled in a way she hoped would ingratiate her to the woman. "Thank you for seeing me. My name is Greta Franklin. I'm hoping you can give me some information about my brother. He is a salesman for Washburn Mills Flour Company, and your lovely store is on his route."

The manager raised her chin and examined Greta. "Are you referring to Emile Franklin?"

"Yes. Didn't I say?" Greta placed her palm on her forehead and feigned embarrassment. "Please forgive me. I've been traveling for such a long time my brain is muddled. You see, we haven't heard from Emile in several months, and my parents are worried sick."

Mrs. Patterson jerked her head to the side, indicating she wanted to move to a quieter location. Greta followed her toward the back of the store. "Emile hasn't called on me since last autumn," Mrs. Patterson said in a quiet voice. "There's a new salesman from Washburn Mills, an older man who can hardly hear. I have to practically shout into his ear when I place my order.”

Greta covered her mouth with one hand. “Oh no. I don’t suppose you know anything about Emile, do you? He must have found another job and decided to relocate. I just wish he’d send a letter home, so we’d know he was all right.”

The manager dropped her voice to a near-whisper. “Are you aware of your brother’s….” Mrs. Patterson glanced to her left and then to her right. “Perhaps the correct word would be *illicit* activities?”

Greta tried to appear shocked. She was aware of Emile’s crimes, all right. “My parents despair over Emile’s lack of morality, but they still worry about him. Did Emile get into trouble while he was in Fort Madison?”

The older lady rolled her eyes. “That would be an understatement. Your brother became involved in a ring of poker players at Lou’s Tavern. It’s a low kind of place near the river. When he got in too deep with the gamblers, he decided to quit his salesman job and move across the state line. You know, Emile is quite the flirt. He even tried to court me, but, when I made it clear I wouldn’t pay his gambling debt, he moved on to a rich widow in New Wexford. The Ansley family owns several grocery stores throughout the state.”

It was so familiar. Emile had taken advantage of yet another lonely woman. He’d probably met her when he’d called at the grocery and set his sights on someone who could rescue him from his mistakes. Poor woman. Greta and Millie would likely have to inform her of Emile’s dishonesty.

“So,” Mrs. Patterson continued, “my best guess is your brother is enjoying the advantages of a rich woman.”

Greta shook her head slowly. “I appreciate your help, ma’am, and I sincerely hope I find him in New Wexford. He has much to answer for.”

Mrs. Patterson patted Greta’s hand. “There’s one in every family. Your mother has my sympathy.”

Greta thought about Emile’s mother. She’d never met the woman, but she also felt sorry for her. Greta stepped away from the counter and turned toward the door. “Thank you again. I need to make my way to the depot and buy a ticket for the next train to New Wexford.”

Mrs. Patterson smiled and nodded. "Have a safe trip, dear."

***

George sat at his desk in the warehouse and stared at Greta's empty chair. She'd been gone for one day, and it was time for her to come back. He didn't usually see her every day, but now that Henry had appointed a foreman to oversee the work, George had more time to devote to managing the building materials and hunting new opportunities for his company. Without his mind crowded with thoughts of work there was plenty of space for Greta. But Greta was gone.

She was fine, he told himself. She was a capable woman who could take care of herself. She didn't need him to hold her hand or protect her. He wanted to do those things and more, but it would have to wait until she returned.

Whenever that was.

When he saw her again, he would hold and kiss her for the first hour, talk to her for the next hour, and plan their future after that. No matter what news she brought back, he'd do whatever was necessary to make her his wife. A woman like Greta came along once in a lifetime. He wasn't about to miss his chance.

Movement in the warehouse caught George's attention. Henry had returned from the worksite and was adding pipes to a stack against one wall. Tired of worrying about Greta and unwilling to tackle the challenges of the worksite, George sauntered into the warehouse and called to Henry. "How do you feel about shopping today?"

Henry's mouth quirked into a sly smile. "What are we buyin'? New dresses or new hats?"

George slipped his hands into his pockets. "Motorized vehicles."

Henry's eyebrows rose. "You don't say! Movin' into the twentieth century, are we?"

"'Bout time, don't you think?"

"I do. Farmer Claywell will be disappointed to find out you're not goin' to need his team of draft horses."

"I already talked to him. Told him after this job, I wouldn't need his horses. They served their purpose, but the big outfits are completely mechanized."

"Yeah," Henry answered with a sigh, "it's the end of an era. Blacksmiths and harness makers better start lookin' for a new line of work. What kind of truck you plannin' on buyin'?"

"Two trucks actually. One able to haul materials from the warehouse to the job site and one for my personal use."

The corners of Henry's mouth curved down as he thought about George's plan. "I think it's a good idea, but who's goin' to teach you how to drive 'em?"

George scowled at the question. "How hard can it be? If my baby brother can drive, it can't be too difficult."

"Well," Henry said with a chuckle, "I guess we'll both learn at the same time. After all, you can't drive two at once, can you?"

"Not even I can manage that."

Two hours later, George maneuvered a new Buick Standard platform truck into the semi-circular drive in front of the warehouse, followed by Henry driving a Ford Model T open truck. After coming to an unsteady stop, George turned off the powerful thirty-seven horsepower motor and climbed out.

Henry stood next to the Ford, shaking his head. George sauntered toward him. "Everything all right?"

"It's a wonder," Henry said. "Didn't think I'd ever get a chance to drive one." He jerked his head toward the larger truck. "How much can we load on that monster?"

"Half-ton," George answered. "And the Ford will be perfect for taking smaller loads."

Henry made a low whistle. "Nine hundred dollars for mine and fifteen hundred for yours. You're in the big time now, my friend."

"I've got big dreams, " George said. "Big dreams need big trucks."

"I guess so. Wait till Greta sees these. Think she'll like 'em?"

George hadn't considered Greta's opinion. She'd trained him to keep track of receipts, but she'd never commented on the items he'd purchased. "Guess we'll find out."

"When's she comin' back?"

"Soon, I hope."

"Yeah, we need her to keep us straight." Henry rubbed his palm against his cheek. "Did you realize that not one worker has complained about a mistake on his paycheck? In all this time, not one complaint. I've *never* gone this long without some carpenter's helper grousin' 'bout gettin' shorted his hours."

"Maybe that's because we pay more than any other jobs around here."

"Don't get me wrong, the men like those fat paychecks. But what I'm talkin' about is Greta's accuracy. I couldn't do what she does. Now, when do I get to drive my new truck again?"

"*Your* new truck?"

Henry barked a laugh. "It's mine when you're not drivin' it."

George appreciated Henry's wit. "Tell you what. Let's load up what we can and drive both trucks to the site. I wouldn't want our employees to miss us too much."

"Yeah," Henry said with an eyeroll. "I 'magine they're just cryin' their eyes out from loneliness."

CHAPTER NINE

The following morning, Greta and Millie stood on the sidewalk and stared at the stately Georgian mansion. "You think this is it?" Millie half-whispered.

"See that sign?" Greta gestured to a painted sign hanging between two brick columns. "Ansley Manor. That's the name the hotel clerk told us, and this is definitely the address you got from Washburn Mills."

"I guess you're right. But still...."

Greta understood Millie's reluctance. The house reminded her of pictures she'd seen of Thomas Jefferson's home. A wide expanse of meticulously mowed green lawn stretched in front of the three-story red brick building. Evenly spaced dormer windows capped the third floor, and a white balustrade crowned the roof.

"Well," Greta said, "are we going or not?"

Millie's feet creeped along the brick walkway that led to a semicircular portico in the center of the house. "Bet they have a butler."

Only rich families in motion pictures had butlers. But Greta hadn't come this far to let the Widow Ansley's butler stop her. She stepped to the door, pulled Millie to join her, and pressed the button for the bell. The seconds crawled by as they waited for someone to answer. Greta could have sworn she felt Millie's nerves vibrating through the narrow space that separated the two.

The door finally opened to reveal a gray-haired woman wearing the black-and-white uniform of a maid. "May I help you?"

Millie slipped behind Greta. Greta gathered her courage. She wouldn't be able to live with herself if she backed down now. "Mrs. Greta Franklin and Mrs. Millie Franklin to call on the lady of the house."

"Please wait here," the maid replied, "and I'll see if Mrs. Ansley is at home."

The maid closed the door with a quiet click. The maid had referred to Mrs. Ansley. Did that mean the widow hadn't married Emile?

"Greta?" Millie whispered.

"Yes?"

"What if she's not home?"

"I think the maid meant she'd find out if Mrs. Ansley wanted to see us. If the lady truly wasn't home, the maid would have told us that first."

"Oh. How do you know?"

"I read it in a book."

The answer seemed to satisfy Millie, but a few seconds later, she spoke again. "Greta?"

"Yes?"

"What if the widow kicks us out?"

"Then we'll leave, I suppose."

"And Emile? I still got to find him."

Greta wanted to calm Millie's nerves, but she couldn't solve all the problems at once. "Let's worry about that when we have to."

Millie seemed to be thinking it over. "Greta?"

"Yes?"

The door reopened, sparing Greta from another one of Millie's anxious concerns. The maid swung the door wider and smiled. "Please come in. Mrs. Ansley will meet you in her study."

Greta followed the woman through a wide hall decorated with highly polished furniture and oil paintings of breathtaking landscapes. Thick rugs muffled their footsteps, adding to the overall silence of the house. Greta felt as though she'd entered a museum more than a home.

The maid stopped at an open doorway and gestured for Greta and Millie to enter. "Make yourselves comfortable. Mrs. Ansley will be in directly."

Greta seated herself on a sofa upholstered in an elegant damask design. Millie sat beside her, so close their shoulders touched. "Move over," Greta whispered.

"What?"

"Move over. I can hardly breathe, and our hostess will think we're strange for sitting so close together."

Millie gave no reply but did move a few inches.

Greta examined the room while she waited. A gilded table with a telephone stood near a sunny window. An exquisite desk set featuring an inkwell, pen tray, and letter opener gave the impression they were seldom used. Portraits hung on the walls, and Greta assumed they were family members or ancestors who had built the Ansley grocery chain into a profitable business.

Millie gasped, and Greta turned to see the cause of her reaction. A beautiful middle-aged woman with red hair walked into the room. "Good morning," she said in tones that spoke of culture and education. "I've been expecting you. Which one of you is Millie Franklin?"

Millie raised her hand as though she feared it would be bitten off.

The red-haired woman smiled warmly. "How do you do? And you must be Greta Franklin."

Greta got to her feet. "Yes ma'am. Are you Mrs. Ansley?"

"I am indeed. Won't you be seated? I've asked for tea and coffee to be served. It should be here any minute."

Mrs. Ansley settled into a large wing-backed chair that matched the couch. Her dress was the latest fashion. Her earrings displayed three stones — one green, one white, and one blue. Three larger stones set in gold hung from a chain around her neck. Greta was no judge of fine jewelry, but she felt certain the lady was flaunting diamonds, emeralds, and sapphires.

"Now then," Mrs. Ansley began, "I assume you've come to find Emile Franklin."

Millie drew in a quick breath and touched Greta's arm. "That's correct," Greta answered. "Are we in the right place?"

"You are indeed," Mrs. Ansley answered. "Emile is not here at the moment, but he should return soon."

"How....?" Millie couldn't finish the rest of her sentence.

Greta asked the question for her. "How did you know we were coming?"

"Two months ago, I held a dinner party to celebrate my marriage to Emile. He had too much wine at dinner, but he was managing well enough. Then, after dinner, he helped himself to my late husband's twelve-year-old scotch. That's when he began to brag about his exploits."

"So...." Greta began, "he told you about us?"

"My idiot husband told me about his first marriage to Millie and about his second marriage to Greta. He also bragged about how he learned to cheat at poker and the many men he'd duped over a hand of cards. The next morning, he had a terrible headache and absolutely no memory of his confession."

Two maids entered the room, each carrying a large silver tray. While they served the beverages and offered small sandwiches and bite-sized sweets, Mrs. Ansley went to her desk and picked up the telephone. "Yes, operator. Connect me with Arthur Holliman's office."

Greta accepted the cup of hot coffee. She certainly hadn't been expecting such a warm welcome, but it was much better than having to inform Emile's third wife of his bigamy. She'd often scolded herself for marrying Emile, but as she watched Mrs. Ansley, Greta wondered why the older woman had fallen for him. Mrs. Ansley was lovely and well off. What had he offered that convinced her to accept his proposal? Widows were often lonely, and Greta certainly knew how hopeless one could feel when loneliness stretched on for months and months. Perhaps Mrs. Ansley's good sense had been muddied by a combination of Emile's charm and her loneliness and, if a woman such as Mrs. Ansley could be fooled, perhaps Greta should forgive herself for believing Emile's cunning nature.

"Good morning, Arthur," their hostess spoke into the telephone. "Lily Ansley speaking...Can you come to lunch today? The ladies I've been expecting called this morning....That's correct...Very well, I'll see you in a few minutes." Mrs. Ansley ended the call and returned to her chair.

"I wasn't sure you'd married Emile," Millie said. "The lady who answered the door called you Mrs. Ansley."

"Ansley is my family's name. When I told my first husband I didn't wish to legally change my name, he had no objections. So, when I married Emile, I made the same decision."

"Why did you…. I mean, why didn't you….?" Millie looked to Greta for help, but Greta declined to speak for her. Millie cleared her throat and tried again. "Why didn't you tell Emile to leave?"

Mrs. Ansley looked down and smoothed her skirt. "One thing my late husband taught me is that wrongdoers always get caught. It may not come as soon as we think it should, but eventually justice catches up with crooked men like Emile. I didn't want him to relocate to some place where none of us could find him, so I gave him a hefty salary for a minor responsibility in the office of Ansley Foods. He thinks he's pulling the wool over my eyes, but the opposite is true."

Did Mrs. Ansley have so much money she could waste it on Emile? Considering the grandeur of her house and the size of her jewels, Greta concluded she did.

Mrs. Ansley placed her elbow on the arm of the chair and rested her head in her hand. "I must say, you two certainly don't resemble the women Emile described."

Greta and Millie looked at each other. "What did he say?" Millie asked.

"He said *you* were quite demanding and had used your good looks to trap him into marriage."

Greta cut her gaze to Millie. Millie was neither beautiful nor plain. Except for her tiny stature, she looked just like every other woman in the country.

"And you, Greta," Mrs. Ansley continued, "were supposed to be a plump spinster who suffered from shyness. I knew he was a bigamist and a liar, but I never realized how blind Emile was. You're both lovely women with the courage to call him to account. It's an honor to meet you."

Greta and Millie looked at each other. Millie covered her mouth with her hand and broke into muffled giggles. Greta looked away, afraid Millie's giggles were infectious.

"Well," said Mrs. Ansley with raised eyebrows and a wide smile, "that wasn't the reaction I was expecting."

"It's just relief," Greta explained. "We didn't know what we would find here. We thought we'd bring terrible, life-changing news. Imagine how we feel to discover not only that you already knew about Emile, but that you may have some kind of plan."

"Oh, I've got a plan all right," Mrs. Ansley said in the same tone the spider must have used when inviting the fly to enter its parlor.

Before Greta could ask for details, the maid returned with a white-haired man dressed in a business suit. "Mr. Holliman, ma'am."

Mrs. Ansley got to her feet and offered her hand to the gentleman. "Thank you for coming so quickly, Arthur."

The gentleman took her hand in his and inclined his head slightly. "I am always at your service, Lily."

Mrs. Ansley slipped her arm into his and guided him to the sofa. She introduced Greta and Millie, then offered him coffee.

Mrs. Ansley resumed her seat, and Mr. Holliman sat in a matching chair near her. "Arthur is my lawyer," she explained. "He knows all about our situation. I've asked him to speak to you."

A lawyer? Greta straightened her back. Perhaps Mr. Holliman could answer her questions.

Mr. Holliman cleared his throat. "I'd like to address Mrs. Millie Franklin first."

Millie moved away from Greta so she could sit closer to the lawyer. "Yes sir?"

"Emile Franklin told Lily he married you first in Edina, Minnesota. My assistant easily located a record of your legal marriage in Hennepin County. Since he abandoned you and your child, it will be quite easy to obtain a divorce. We will ask for monthly payments of child support, but you should know there is no legal way to force him to pay it."

"Do you want to divorce Emile?" Mrs. Ansley asked.

"Oh yes," Millie answered. "But I need money for my son."

"We'll get to that later," Mrs. Ansley said. "Now Arthur, what about Greta Franklin?"

The lawyer shifted his gaze to Greta. "Since Emile married you and Lily without obtaining a divorce from Millie, your marriages are null and void. In the eyes of the law, you were never married. Therefore, you have no need for a divorce."

"I'm free of him?" Greta asked.

"Free as the proverbial bird," Mr. Holliman answered.

Greta fell back against the sofa. Her marriage had never existed? She'd chastised herself and lived with shame all these months, and it had never happened? No, that was the wrong way to think of it. She'd married Emile in good faith. She'd fulfilled all that was expected of a wife because she'd believed she was lawfully wed. Emile had known their marriage was a fraud, but she hadn't.

"Mr. Franklin has returned, ma'am."

Greta's thoughts had flown like dried autumn leaves, but she gathered them in time to see the maid standing in the doorway.

"Ask him to join us," Mrs. Ansley instructed.

As the maid left the room, Millie looked at Greta. Greta looked at Mrs. Ansley. "Another part of your plan?"

Mrs. Ansley's eyes lit, but her smile was cold. "We've arrived at the best part."

Greta got to her feet and stared at the empty doorway. In a few minutes, or seconds, Emile would walk into the room. What should she do? Stay and confront him? Run?

Millie slipped behind Greta and wrapped her arms around Greta's waist. Greta felt the small woman's desperate trembling and put her arm around Millie's shoulder.

A man dressed in a brown suit with a yellow vest entered the room. His two-tone shoes were polished to a high gleam, and his dark hair was cut in the latest style. Greta studied the man. Was this Emile? The man she'd married wore a shabby black suit with a frayed collar.

But Greta didn't have long to determine the man's identity. In a matter of seconds, Millie transformed from a frightened kitten to a vicious tigress. She sprang from her spot and landed on Emile's back. "You dirty cheat!" she screamed, pounding his back with her fists. "Of all the lowdown, rotten schemes!"

Emile struggled to get the harridan off him, but Millie had years of anger to expel. "You have a son, you rat! A child!"

Millie slid down Emile's back and landed on her rear end. Emile held out his hands in a gesture of supplication, but Mrs. Ansley and Mr. Holliman crossed their arms in front of their bodies.

Millie jumped to her feet and slapped Emile's face. "You said you loved me!" She hit his head with her open hand. "You said you were proud of Joey!" She used both hands to shove his chest, forcing Emile to rock backwards. "You're nothing but a snake in the grass!"

Emile leaned against the wall, his fine suit now crumpled, his slicked-back hair now hanging in his face. His gaze darted from Millie to Greta to Mrs. Ansley and back again. Millie stood over him, her face red from the exertion and her chest rising and falling with angry breaths.

Greta's heart went out to Millie. Not only had Emile betrayed her, he'd left her with a child to raise. Greta hadn't needed to face her parents' disapproval because she didn't have a child, but Millie had to live with it every day. Greta approached Millie, touched her shoulders, and turned her around. Then she guided Millie back to the sofa. "Nicely done," Greta said quietly.

Mrs. Ansley walked to her desk, poured a glass of water from a crystal pitcher, and carried it to Emile.

"How did you know?" Emile asked after draining the glass.

"In vino veritas," Mrs. Ansley answered.

Milled nudged Greta with her shoulder. "What did she say?"

Greta kept her gaze fixed on Emile. "In wine, there is truth."

"Did you learn that in a book too?"

Greta nodded.

Emile's expression transformed from confusion to surrender. It seemed as though he knew he'd been caught and there was no escape. "What do you want, Lily?"

"Come and sit down. Mr. Holliman has a few things to say to you " Mrs. Ansley returned to her chair.

Emile stood, straightened his clothing, brushed back his disheveled hair, and approached the group. The only empty seat was on the sofa beside Millie, but he sidestepped her and retrieved a chair from the desk.

Mr. Holliman scooted to the edge of his seat. "Bigamy is a crime in this state, Mr. Franklin. It is punishable by up to five years in prison. Mrs. Ansley is ready to press charges and testify in court against you. There is little doubt about your guilt. The prosecutor need only produce the county records of your three marriages and zero divorces."

Emile shifted in his chair and swallowed.

"Mrs. Ansley has several conditions for you to consider in lieu of facing prosecution," Mr. Holliman continued.

Emile cut his gaze to Mrs. Ansley. Her face had turned to stone, showing no hint of emotion.

"First," the lawyer said, "you will sign a divorce agreement with Millie Franklin. Second, you will keep your current position at Ansley Foods, but your wages will be garnished in the amount of twenty dollars each month. That amount will be sent to Millie Franklin for child support until your son turns twenty-one years of age."

Emile began to bluster. "But...but...I only make fifty dollars a month."

"Far above the average salary," Mr. Holliman answered patiently. "However, Mrs. Ansley intends to raise your pay."

Emile glanced at Mrs. Ansley, but she did not react.

"Third," the lawyer continued, "you will remove all of your belongings from this house. However, if you leave town or quit your job, you will be found and prosecuted to the full extent of the law."

Emile brushed his trouser leg and cocked his head. "So I'll be in a different kind of prison. I *have* to keep working, and I *have* to live in New Wexford." Emile made a dismissive sound. "I don't see how you can make me."

Mr. Holliman's tone didn't change, but his face took on the demeanor of an executioner. "Your crimes have been uncovered, Mr. Franklin, and you *will* pay for them. One way or the other."

Emile shook his head and smiled in a way that made Greta's skin crawl. "What harm did I do?" he simpered. "Paid attention to three lonely women? Gave them hope for romance where none existed before?"

Mr. Holliman got to his feet. He was no longer detached and business-like. Emile's feeble excuses had obviously angered him. "You took advantage of three respectable women! You abandoned a child! Personally, I'd like to see you in the state penitentiary, but then your child would have no hope of financial support."

The lawyer stood over Emile, his hands clenched into fists, his expression as hard as granite.

Emile tugged at his shirt collar and swallowed. After recovering from Millie's attack, he'd played the part of the calm, collected gentleman, but Mr. Holliman's threats must have shaken that facade.

"Seeing that I have no choice in the matter," Emile said, "I will comply. If you'll excuse me, I'll go and pack my things."

"It's been done for you," Mrs. Ansley said, her back rigid and her voice as cold as icicles. "You'll find a trunk in your bedroom."

Emile gazed straight ahead, as though fearing to make eye contact with anyone in the room and strode out of the study.

As soon as he was out of sight, Mrs. Ansley slumped in her chair. Mr. Holliman collapsed into his seat and rested his forehead in his hand.

Millie was bright-eyed and smiling. "When can I get that divorce?"

Mr. Holliman managed a weak smile. "The papers have already been drawn up. I'll get Mr. Franklin's signature tomorrow. Then, after you sign, I'll submit them to the court. Abandonment is one cause the judge never opposes."

Millie seemed to be satisfied by his answer, but Greta had her doubts. "You know, there's very little chance Emile will comply. He's not the kind of man who shoulders responsibility."

"To say the least," Mrs. Ansley concurred.

"That's why I intend to get his signature tomorrow," Mr. Holliman said. "Who knows how long he'll actually show up to work?"

"I'll tell you one thing," Millie said, "if I had a job like his, I'd show up every day and twice on Saturdays."

Mrs. Ansley turned her gaze on Millie. "Really? Because you know, my dear, that can be easily accomplished."

Every part of Millie's body came to attention. "I'd love to get away from my hometown. The gossips there are deadly! You should hear what they say about me raising my boy by myself." Millie rolled her eyes.

"Since we all agree it's highly unlikely for Emile to do the right thing," Mrs. Ansley continued, "offering you his job seems like the obvious solution. You could earn his salary and wouldn't need his monthly support."

Millie leaned so far forward her body was only inches away from dropping off the sofa. "I don't know what Emile's job is, ma'am, but I give you my word I'll learn it and do the best I can."

Mrs. Ansley finally smiled. "I have no doubt. You and your son are welcome to stay here until you find a place of your own."

Millie gave a quick squeal of happiness and covered her face with her hands. Greta blinked at Mrs. Ansley. Was there no end to her generosity? Why would she offer Millie a way to stand on her own two feet after what Emile had done?

Because Mrs. Ansley understood, Greta realized. Somewhere in her life, Mrs. Ansley had been in a situation where she needed unconditional help. Now, she was in a position to give a helping hand. It seemed as though being judgmental disappeared when empathy entered.

Mrs. Ansley looked at Greta. "What about you? Now that you know you're free of Emile, what are your plans?"

"I have a position as a bookkeeper at two businesses in Brightfield," Greta answered. "I'm very happy there, and I will return on tomorrow's train."

"I'm glad to hear it," Mrs. Ansley said. "You're still a young woman, Greta. You're attractive, intelligent, and gainfully employed. Your future is bright, but if you ever need my help, please let me know. Women can so easily become the victims of men's duplicity. We must help each other when possible."

Greta's heart went out to Mrs. Ansley. She was a rich and powerful woman, but she'd been fooled by Emile as well. "Thank you, ma'am."

Mrs. Ansley tapped the arms of her chair with her palms. "Now then, let's have lunch. I'm sure Cook is fuming because I've delayed so long."

Mr. Holliman stood and offered his arm to Mrs. Ansley. Greta and Millie followed the pair out of the study and into a lavish dining room where a long table with four place settings of beautiful china waited.

Millie pulled Greta to the side. "Unless you object, I won't go back with you tomorrow. I want to know more about my new job, and I want to write a letter to my family."

Greta put her hands on Millie's arms and looked down at her. "You're sure about this?"

"Heavens no," Millie said with a laugh. "But it's a way to be on my own, not depending on my family or on Emile, and it's a way to make a fresh start. There's a lot more good than bad about the offer."

"You're a brave woman, Millie."

"Oh, not really, but I can be brave for Joey. He deserves the best future I can give him, and New Wexford looks a lot brighter than Edina. I couldn't have done any of this without your help."

"Me? I haven't done anything."

"You welcomed me instead of throwing me out, you helped me find Emile, and you were a friend when I needed one. I dreaded telling you about my marriage, but …. Maybe it's turned out all right."

Hope shone in Millie's eyes. How could Greta discourage her? "I think it's worth a try. If it doesn't work out, you could always find something else."

"That's true." Millie placed the palm of her hand on her midriff. "Now that it's all over, I'm starving!"

Greta's stomach churned and shuddered. Thoughts of food disgusted her, but insulting Mrs. Ansley by rejecting her food was unthinkable. She would sit at Mrs. Ansley's elegant table and do her best.

CHAPTER TEN

George hadn't been able to stop smiling since he'd received Greta's telegram. She'd written her arrival time and two very important words. *Good news.* She must be free from that heartless husband. And, she was coming back to him!

He checked the station clock. The station master had reassured him the train was on time, so she should arrive in a few minutes. He paced the platform, his gaze fixed on the southbound tracks. Where was that train?

He had plans for the day. He couldn't be alone with her if he took her to his parents' house, and her boarding house was out of the question. No man was allowed to visit a single woman in her room. The warehouse was a place of business and not conducive to the romance he hoped to create, but he had a plan. All he needed was Greta.

George counted his steps. When he reached seventy-six, he heard the sound he'd been waiting for — the unmistakable whistle of the steam locomotive and the metallic squeal of brakes. Greta had arrived. Finally.

His hungry gaze searched the crowd exiting the passenger car, but he couldn't locate her. When Greta finally stepped off the train and aimed her lovely smile at him, George hurried to her side, took her bag, and fought the urge to embrace her. As far as the citizens of Brightfield knew, Greta was his employee. It wouldn't raise too many eyebrows if he was seen meeting a train or simply giving her a ride but acting on his romantic impulses would sully her reputation.

He removed his hat and bent down to speak into her ear. "I'm glad you're back."

Her face was flushed, and her eyes shone. "So am I. I have so much to tell you."

Restraining his embrace was growing painful. "I can't wait to hear it. I have several surprises for you."

She cocked her gaze up to him. "Good surprises?"

"I hope so."

George led her to the street and stopped beside his light-duty truck. "What's this?" Greta asked as she admired the vehicle.

"This is surprise number one." George opened the passenger door and waited for her to enter. "Bought this one and a heavy-duty truck for the business. It's at the warehouse."

Greta ran her hand over the dashboard. "It's perfect! Just right for work or everyday transportation. I didn't know you could drive."

George stored her travel bag in the bed of the truck and got behind the steering wheel. "Oh, I've been driving for at least two days now."

"Two days?" Greta asked with a laugh. "Who taught you?"

"The salesman. It's really not so hard. Once I figured out the clutch and how to change gears, it was a piece of cake."

George pulled away from the railway station and headed toward the work site. As soon as he was on the road, he reached for Greta's hand. "Missed you."

She squeezed his hand. "I thought about you the whole time."

"So...you're free, Greta? Free to marry me?"

"I'm not married, and, according to a lawyer I spoke to in New Wexford, I never was."

George nodded and focused on the road. It was enough. Once they were alone, once he was free to hold her, he'd want to know more. But for now, her presence at his side was enough.

***

Where there had once been a sad gathering of rundown shacks, two newly constructed houses stood. "George!" Greta said with a gasp. "You've already finished another one?"

Pride shone brightly in his smile. "We sure did. Even though it's bigger, we got it up faster. It'll be ready for the next family in a few days."

Greta got out of his truck and walked from one side of the new house to the other. "It's so big!"

George thrust his hands into his trouser pockets and rocked back on his heels. "Four bedrooms in this place. One downstairs and three up." George led her onto the covered porch and opened the front door.

Greta was speechless as she turned first one way and then the other to see all the fine details of the empty rooms. Every entryway was crowned with wide molding stained and varnished to its natural hue. Built-in bookcases bracketed a large window, and a window seat had been added between them. She squatted in front of the wide fireplace centered along an interior wall. "I just can't believe how perfect everything is."

"Come upstairs," George said, extending his hand. "I have something for you."

Curiosity sparked Greta's interest, and she slipped her hand in his. He followed her up the sturdy staircase and guided her down a hall and into a back bedroom. On the floor, she saw a folded blanket with a basket beside it. "What's this?"

"A way to be alone with you." George pulled her into his arms and kissed her.

Greta sank into his embrace. She was home. Everything right, everything safe, everything loving existed within this man.

When he ended the kiss, he leaned his head toward the wide window at the back of the room. "Look at this."

The spring sun had dipped close to the horizon, transforming the sky to soft hues of violet and pink. From the second-floor window, Greta looked over a meadow full of white trillium and woodland violets. The wildflowers seemed to catch each ray of dying light, holding that life-giving power close to their breasts before surrendering to the evening. "Oh," she whispered reverentially. "Sometimes the world is so beautiful, it's hard not to cry."

"Cry all you want," George said in a tender voice, "as long as they're not tears of sadness."

Greta leaned against his broad, strong chest. "It's like you and I are the only humans in the world. The fairies are going to sleep, the stars are beginning their night watch, and only you and I are awake to bear witness."

She closed her eyes and breathed in his clean, masculine scent. A few months earlier, she'd been alone and ashamed, but hope had replaced her shame, and love had erased her loneliness.

"I brought dinner," George said as he stepped away from the window and spread out the blanket so that it edged one wall. "Sit here, and I'll show you what I packed."

"You thought of everything," Greta said as she eased herself onto the floor.

"Best place I could think of where no one would bother us. Everything in this house is ready except the electricity. And the furniture, of course."

"Furniture?"

George removed two wrought-iron candle holders from the basket and placed them at the far corners of the blanket. "Hildy watched the first family move into their new home and was surprised they had so few belongings. She's contracted Purcell's Furniture Emporium to provide the basics that will stay with the house when the tenants move."

Greta shook her head in wonder. "Hildy is an incredibly generous woman. At first, I felt intimidated by her — so rich, so pretty, so polished — but now…"

George reached into his jacket, withdrew a box of matches, and lowered himself to one knee to light the candles. "She and my mother have been friends for a long time, and she was always around the house for holidays and Sunday lunches. Then Andrew, my *baby* brother, told us he planned to marry her!"

Greta laughed at his obvious incredulity. "Did your family object?"

George placed one hand on the wall and lowered himself to the blanket so that his back rested against it. "When Andrew told us about his plans to marry Hildy, there were a few seconds of stunned silence. He hadn't said a word to us about his feelings for her. But after the shock wore off, we were glad to have her officially join the family. To me, Hildy was just another one of my mother's friends. She's a few years older than me, a few million dollars richer, and lives in the nicest house in town. But the more I get to know Hildy, the more I understand what Andrew sees in her." He reached into the basket and removed a small bouquet of wildflowers. "I didn't pick too many," he promised.

Greta's surprise was two-fold. Not only had his small gift been unexpected, but the thought of George stooping to pick wild sunflowers and red clover astonished her. He was a busy man — a hard-working, muscular, extremely masculine man — but he'd taken the time and trouble to pick flowers. Beneath his brawn beat a tender heart. A heart she would treasure and protect. She kissed his cheek. "They're lovely. Thank you."

"Now," George said, slapping his hands on his knees, "it's time for food." He withdrew several small plates from the basket. "I brought slices of chicken, tomatoes, cheese, and bread. Will they do?"

"Of course," Greta replied, helping him set the towel-covered saucers on the blanket. "I've never had an indoor picnic before."

"Oh!" George snapped his fingers. "There are also two bottles of Coca Cola." He produced the last items in the basket.

"Do you have an opener?"

George squeezed his eyes shut. "I knew I was forgetting something. Oh, wait." He stood, reached into the pocket of his trousers, and withdrew his pocketknife. "This will work." He opened the largest blade, braced the bottle against his thigh, and pried off the top. "Nothing to it," he proclaimed as he handed the open bottle to Greta.

Handsome, tender-hearted, strong, and able to solve problems with a pocketknife. She'd be crazy to let such a man slip away.

"Now then," George said as he sat down beside her, "tell me about your trip."

Greta told him everything, pausing occasionally to take a bite or answer a question, but including every detail she could recall. George listened attentively, his expression changing to show outrage or concern, but interrupting only to ask for clarification.

"I didn't recognize Emile when he walked in the room," Greta said with a shake of her head. "He had changed so much. Like those lizards that change their skin color based on where they are."

"Lizard is a good description of that guy," George said with disgust. "He's definitely cold-hearted."

"And you should have seen Millie!" Greta burst into giggles. "She slapped him so hard I expected him to spit out loose teeth."

George laughed with her. "Guess my fists weren't needed after all."

Greta sighed and wiped the mirthful tears from her eyes. "I fully expect Emile will disappear. He used to talk about escaping to the New Mexico territory and changing his identity. I pity the next woman who falls for his rubbish."

George slid his arm across her shoulders and pulled her closer. "Not your problem anymore. His first wife landed in a better position, and so have you."

Greta widened her eyes. "That's for sure."

"You're a mighty brave woman, Greta."

She didn't deserve his praise. Hadn't she spent most of her life fearful of rejection and isolation? "I've never thought of myself that way."

"Only a brave woman would have confronted that dragon and slayed him. Now that you're back, I'd like to discuss our future."

Greta looked up at him. Although she appreciated his support, there were some smaller dragons she had to face. "I'm hoping you still want to court me."

George squeezed her shoulder against his chest. "How can you doubt it?"

She hid her face in his chest. She didn't want to confess the mountain of insecurities she'd lived with every day of her life. She was changing. For all the pain Emile had brought into her life, he'd also spurred her into action. She'd stood up for herself for the first time in her life. With that victory in her pocket, she could face more battles.

George kissed her forehead. "How long are you going to make me wait, Greta?"

"Wait to court me?"

"Wait to marry you."

"You're so sure?"

"Every time I'm near you, I have to fight my desire to make you my mate. I want everything with you. I want a home, children, a profitable business. Everything with you at my side."

Greta was quiet. Everything she'd ever wanted, offered to her with love. How could this be real?

"Nothing to say?" George prompted.

"I want the same," she whispered.

"But?"

"Maybe I'm asking for too much…"

He waited for her to finish, but the words were trapped beneath layers of fear. "What is it?" he prompted.

"I want to have a real wedding."

George's eyebrows drew together. "Isn't that what I'm offering?"

"Yes, I mean no. Well, not exactly " Greta shook her head as if to erase her false start. "You want to marry as soon as possible, but I did it all wrong the last time. Now I want to do it the right way."

The confused expression on George's face hadn't changed. "You'd better spell it out for me."

Greta scooted away so that she could explain herself without being affected by his nearness. "I accepted Emile's proposal because I thought he'd be my only chance. We went to the courthouse two days after I agreed. My parents disapproved, I didn't have a wedding, and I wore my best church dress. This time, when I marry the *right* man, I want to do it the *right* way."

George nodded slowly. "I think I understand. You want to do it the traditional way. A church wedding, a fancy dress, and a party for our friends and families."

"That's right," she answered eagerly. "And, if he'll go along with it, I'd like my father to give me away."

George extended his bottom lip as he thought it over. "I think it's a grand idea."

She clapped her hands together. "You do? Really?"

George's acceptance of her wishes was evident in his wide smile and shining eyes. "I really do. What do we do first?"

"Tell your family, I suppose. They think I'm a married woman."

"Hm...best time to do that is Sunday lunch. My whole family will be there. Then, we'll take a trip to visit your folks."

Greta knew it was necessary, but telling her parents was one step she dreaded.

"And after we talk to our families," George continued, "we'd better talk to Reverend Hixson."

Greta covered her face with both hands and groaned.

George's expression darkened with concern. "What is it sweetheart?"

"I totally forgot about the church," Greta said in a near-whisper. "Everyone there thinks I'm married. We can't just have a wedding without explaining it to them." Greta buried her head in her hands. "I dread dealing with the gossips."

"You confronted the man who took advantage of your innocence, you're going to face my family and yours, but you're afraid of a few old women who have nothing better to do than spread malicious rumors?"

How could she make him understand? He had grown up so differently than she. "I know it may sound ridiculous, but when you've spent your life trying to live up to someone else's ideals, having their approval can be the most important thing of all."

George adjusted his position so that he faced her. "Sounds to me as though you've misplaced that importance."

Irritation flared in her chest. "I don't expect you to understand. You weren't born a girl. You didn't grow up with expectations you'd never fulfill."

George waved his hand in front of his chest, as though brushing away the crumbs of her discontent. "I don't want to argue now. It's getting late, and I need to take you home. But we'll get everything ironed out. I'm not giving up on you."

***

The next morning, Henry sat at Greta's desk in the warehouse and examined the artist's rendition of the renovated hospital. "You sure you want to tackle a job this big?"

"It's just one wing of the hospital," George argued. "A separate area for pediatric patients."

Henry rubbed one whiskered cheek. "Still, it's different from buildin' houses. This is three stories, lots of specifications, and lots of headaches."

"And lots of money." The hospital addition would require a significant outlay for George, but it would allow him to keep all his employees. "So, now that you've told me why I shouldn't do it, tell me how to submit a bid."

Henry's cheeks puffed out as he exhaled. "Let's see the blueprints the architect gave you."

"They're only on loan," George said, rolling out the plans on the surface of his desk. "I have to return them in a few days."

Henry offered a wry grin. "I hope you bought a new notebook. The first step is to list the materials we'll need to purchase, and that alone might take up the whole thing. Is Greta back yet?"

George kept his gaze on the blueprints. "She returned yesterday afternoon. Why?"

"We're goin' to need her help with the price of materials. Not to mention you're in a better mood when she's here. Somethin' tells me you might be sweet on her."

George didn't try to hide his smile. "Think so?"

"Yeah, I think so. You look like a little boy with a new puppy whenever you're near her, and you spend more time in this office than on the job site."

"You have everything under control out there. Making Vincent Dowling a foreman was one of your best ideas. He's as dependable as sweat in August."

Henry chuckled and leaned back in his chair. "If this hospital bid doesn't work out, you might consider buyin' some land and buildin'

101

more houses. People been stoppin' by and askin' if we're goin' to sell the ones we're buildin'."

George had already thought about that possibility, but he wanted Mason Construction to build a reputation in the construction industry. Branching out from family homes was the next logical step. "Since Hildy paid for the house blueprints, would I need to get her permission or give her part of the profit?"

Henry shrugged. "Good question. Either talk to her or buy blueprints of your own. You've made a profit on this job, haven't you?"

George knew his bank balance but hadn't yet projected how far that money would stretch. "I need to ask Greta where I stand. Whatever profit I make will be put into the next venture."

"The hospital will advance you some funds." Henry gestured to the blueprint. "Big jobs like this usually pay half up front, and the second half when everythin' is finished."

George hadn't known that detail. It was another reason to win the hospital contract. "If I buy land and build a whole new neighborhood, I'd need my own money."

"Or an investor. You're steppin' in big business when you start fishin' for investors."

Big business was exactly where George wanted his company to be. "What time is it?" Henry asked.

George withdrew his pocket watch from his vest. "Almost one o'clock. Greta ought to be here soon."

Henry's normally jovial countenance darkened. "Maybe this ain't none of my business, but don't it bother you she's a married woman?"

George looked Henry in the eye. "Of course, but the thing is, she's not."

"She's not what? Not married?"

George hesitated before giving Henry the details. He hadn't told his family yet, and it seemed disloyal for Henry to know before they did. "Keep this under your hat, all right?"

"You have my word."

George took a deep breath and let it out. "Greta found out the man she married is a bigamist. Her marriage wasn't legal."

Henry's expression veered sharply to outrage. "What? How could someone do that to our Greta? She's nothin' but sweetness and loyalty."

George had known he could count on Henry's fondness for Greta. "Don't ask me, but if I ever meet the guy, it'll be hard not to rearrange his face."

"Yeah, and when you're finished with him, I wouldn't mind gettin' in a few punches."

"Consider it a deal."

CHAPTER ELEVEN

As she set the table on Sunday afternoon, Greta kept one eye on Hildy. There was no reason to be so nervous. Helen Mason was her friend. Abigail was her friend. And Hildy was….? Polite. Kind. Generous. But no matter how amiable Hildy was, Greta couldn't rid herself of the insecurity that plagued her whenever Hildy walked into the room.

It was a familiar feeling. Greta hadn't known something was wrong with her until her schoolmates had begun to tease her for being as tall as a giraffe and as strong as a boy. From that point on, she'd been crippled by self-consciousness. Her mother was petite and delicate, and her father, only a head taller than her mother, had always been a bantamweight. As she'd continued to grow throughout her adolescence, her mother's criticism had escalated, but try as she might, Greta couldn't make herself into a dainty, elfin girl.

As the other girls married and had children, Greta's jealousy had intensified. Why had she been overlooked and rejected when less intelligent and less capable girls had been chosen? What did the petite girls have that Greta didn't? The envy ate at her confidence, and bit-by-bit, Greta had retreated into herself. She'd kept her father's accounts and helped in the grocery, and she'd assisted her mother with housework. As her friends married and became busy with husbands and children, Greta had endured the loneliness of not being one of the chosen. She'd fought against bitterness daily, determined to hold on to the fantasy of hope.

And then Emile had proposed.

Greta sighed deeply as she set the last plate on the table and stepped back to regard Hildy and Abigail. They looked just like the classic beauties Greta's mother had held up as the feminine ideal. Abigail was a beautiful blonde with a creamy complexion and an athletic body. Hildy was a slender brunette who walked as lithely as a dancer. It had been difficult for Greta to be with them and not feel inadequate and awkward. But Abigail had resolved to make Greta her friend and had finally won her over with unceasing kindness.

If Greta married George, these two women would become her sisters-in-law. It was time for her to overcome the uneasiness she felt whenever Hildy was nearby.

"Everything's ready," Helen said as she looked at the table. "Where are the boys?"

"Outside," Abigail answered, "admiring George's truck. Want me to call them?"

Before Helen could answer, the screen door squeaked open, and Simon Mason led the other men into the kitchen. "I smell something delicious."

"I knew you'd come in when you got hungry," Helen said with a grin. "Now, everyone wash up and take your seats."

When they were all seated and the blessing had been recited, Simon scanned the table. "Who's going to share their news first? I've been warned not to ask John about wedding plans, so….?"

John sent a baleful glare toward his father.

Abigail spoke up first. "My new kittens are having a great time in our house."

"What did you name them?" Helen asked.

"I'm calling mine Smoky, but I don't know what Greta wants to name hers. Any ideas, Greta?"

Greta frowned in confusion. "You have a kitten for me?"

"I forgot to tell you," George said. "With so much going on, it's been hard to keep up with everything."

"Don't worry," Abigail hastened to reassure her. "The kittens just arrived yesterday, and I'm already in love with both of them. If you decide you don't want him, your kitten is welcome to stay with his brother."

"It's not that I don't want to have a kitten," Greta said, "but who knows how long it will be until I have a place to keep him."

George's brother, John, had an impish glint in his eyes. "What about you, Benjamin? Do you like having two kittens?"

Benjamin grinned and shook his head. "John, John, John. When will you learn? If two mischievous kittens make Abigail happy, then I'm happy."

Simon and Andrew laughed along with Benjamin. "John's day is coming," George's father said. "We're not allowed to talk to him about his fiancée or his wedding, but someday he'll be a husband too."

"What about Siva?" Greta asked.

Abigail leaned forward and looked at Greta with a perplexed expression. "Siva? For the kitten?"

"That's right," Greta clarified. "My parents speak Croatian, and Siva is the word for gray."

Abigail's expression changed from puzzled to enchanted. "Oh, how lovely. It's perfect."

"I like it too," Hildy said. "I've always wanted to learn another language."

"Oh, I don't really speak Croatian," Greta protested. "I only know a few words."

"Smokey and Siva," George's mother announced. "Sounds like they go together."

With that matter settled, the other members of the family reported their news. Andrew had been put in charge of the sports stories featured in *The Brightfield Gazette*. Hildy had read about a biplane landing on a naval ship and predicted that the military would soon be buying airplanes. "Time to invest in aviation," she advised. John had planted the corn and oats and expected to put in potatoes next. Finally, Simon called on George.

George glanced at Greta before answering. "Greta and I have some news."

Everyone turned their gazes toward them. Greta felt their expectation like a suspended guillotine blade.

"Well?" Simon commanded in a gruff voice. "Out with it!"

George cleared his throat. "Greta and I are getting married."

Abigail clapped her hands together in front of her chest. "Wonderful!"

Hildy sprang from her chair and put her arms around Greta's shoulders. "I'm so glad. Congratulations!"

Simon and Helen had their heads together at the end of the table, and John continued eating as though nothing special had happened.

But once the excitement had subsided, Andrew asked the question Greta had been dreading. "Isn't Greta already married?"

Andrew's question hushed everyone. George's family needed an explanation. They deserved an explanation. George looked at Greta, silently asking which one of them would give it.

"I thought I was married," Greta began. She took a deep, fortifying breath, and shared her story. She didn't omit the shock she'd felt when Millie had shown up or the shame she'd had to overcome when Emile had abandoned her. She included the happier ending Millie had found because of the kindness of Emile's third wife and the information she'd received from the lawyer.

No one interrupted her. No one ridiculed her. There were looks of incredulity and sympathy, but her worst fears were not realized. No one berated her for bad judgment or for misrepresenting herself as a married woman.

"Despite everything," she concluded, "I'm glad it happened. I wouldn't have found George if I hadn't come to Brightfield, and I wouldn't have come to Brightfield if I hadn't married Emile."

George's mother stood and pulled Greta into an embrace. "You'll make such a good match for George."

"You sure you want him?" Abigail asked with a laugh. "He eats as much as two husbands!"

"I'm sure," Greta said above the laughter.

Dr. Connor offered his hand. "Congratulations. You've found a wonderful new family."

"Thank you." Dr. Connor had treated her headaches by seeing inside her heart. His belief in her had set her on the path to happiness.

"Have you set a date?" George's father asked.

"Not yet," George answered. "We need to tell Greta's parents and talk to Reverend Hixson. Until those things are taken care of, I'd appreciate it if you all would keep this quiet."

"Understood," several family members answered. Others simply nodded their agreement.

"You know," Hildy said, "it sounds like the wedding date won't be soon, so I think a shopping trip is in order. I'd love to take you ladies to my favorite shop."

Abigail gasped audibly. "Shopping? When? Where?"

Hildy's broad smile showed her excitement. "We all need new dresses for a spring wedding. Don't you agree?"

"With matching hats!" Abigail added. "And, of course, we should shop for Greta's wedding dress."

"Oh, I couldn't," Greta protested. "I mean, I'd like to have a wedding dress, but there's time for me to make one."

"Don't steal the fun," Abigail protested. "I've admired Hildy's fashions for so long, and here's the perfect excuse to find out where she buys them."

While Abigail and Hildy talked about fashion and the newest hat styles, Greta leaned closer to George and spoke so that only he could hear. "What do you think about Hildy's invitation?"

"As long as I don't have to go shopping with you, I think it sounds fine. Go and have fun. Buy a wedding dress. Buy ten new dresses with matching hats if that's what you'd like."

Greta rolled her eyes at the thought of ten new dresses. She'd never owned more than three at one time. "We'll see," was all she said.

***

George had reserved a private compartment for the trip to Greta's hometown. The excursion to New Canaan would only last a few hours, but he jumped at any chance to be alone with her. Every day he spent with her cemented his decision to make her his companion for life.

Traveling in private would also quiet some of the town gossips who thought it peculiar that Greta worked with men. She was afforded some leeway when she worked in Benjamin's office. He was a married man, his wife was usually a few steps away, and his patients could easily see what she was doing every time they stepped into the clinic. Working for him, however, was a different story.

After the clinic closed, Greta walked alone to the warehouse office where she worked with him, or Henry, or any number of men who ferried materials to and from the storage site. She was young, attractive, and there was no husband in sight. People who enjoyed making trouble had already caused eyebrows to raise. But what more could he do? Hire an older woman to chaperone Greta? That seemed like a preposterous idea. Besides, once they were married, the whispers would stop. Many wives worked alongside their husbands in the family business. Greta would be no different.

They planned to return later that night, so Greta carried only her handbag and a small sack with gifts for her parents. George stored it in the upper rack of their compartment and stepped into the passageway so Greta would have plenty of space to settle herself. She removed her light overcoat and hung it from a nearby hook. Once she was seated on the forward-facing bench seat, George entered.

Intent on making a good impression, he'd donned his Sunday suit that morning, but he took the first opportunity to remove his hat and jacket and loosen his tie. Benjamin and Andrew stayed in business apparel all day long, but they didn't climb ladders, walk rooflines, or

108

hoist heavy loads. He was most comfortable in work clothes that allowed movement, withstood rough treatment, and were easily cleaned.

As soon as he sat down, George stretched his long legs across the compartment and rested his feet against the bottom of the facing bench. "That's better," he said with a sigh. "Whenever I sit in a passenger coach, I have to fold up like a Jacob's ladder."

"I haven't seen one of those in a long time," Greta said with a chuckle, "but I'm sure you're too big to be a child's toy."

He took a few moments to examine Greta from the corner of his eye. She appeared to be her usual composed self. Her clothing was spotless, her hair was arranged in its normal neat style, and she took his hand without hesitation. But he sensed something under that placid exterior. In a few hours, she'd face her parents, tell them the truth about her marriage, and introduce him. Who wouldn't be uneasy?

"Are you doing all right?" he asked.

Greta leaned her head against his shoulder. "Better than I expected. I know my parents won't approve. Standing up to one's parents is not easy."

Such an idea had never occurred to George. His parents had always wanted what was best for him. Why would he need to stand up to them? Greta said he couldn't understand because he hadn't been born a girl, but, since there was nothing he could do about that, he'd decided to trust her to take care of it. Despite her occasional lapses into uncertainty, Greta struck him as a person who could solve problems and carry on despite difficulties. "What about your father?"

Greta looked out the window. "He doesn't usually say much. My father controls the grocery, and my mother is the boss of the house. I love my parents so much, but I haven't always understood their actions."

"It's hard to remember our parents had a life before us," George said. "Their experiences and personalities were formed long before we showed up." Greta nodded slowly but did not reply. George ran his thumb over the thin gold wedding band she wore on her left hand. "When are you going to take this off?"

"Right now," she announced. "It's so small, I forget it's there." She twisted the band until it slipped off her finger. "I don't think it's very valuable."

"That green stain on your finger tells me you may be right. Isn't that usually a sign of inferior metal?"

Greta shrugged. "I don't know, but it's as fake as Emile was. What do I do with it now?"

"Give it to me." She dropped the ring into his open palm. "I'll throw it in the lake. Or the river. Or the trash."

Greta chuckled. "Throw away the ring. Throw away Emile. Out with the bad, in with the good."

"I'll get you the biggest ring the jeweler has," George promised. "What kind of gemstone would you like?"

"Oh, I don't want a big, gaudy thing that will get in the way when I do housework. And I definitely don't want to worry about an expensive ring being lost or stolen. Your mother, and Abigail, and even Hildy wear simple gold bands. That works for me."

"Consider it done."

The train's whistle blew loud and long, a signal their journey was beginning. As the locomotive pulled out of the station, George stretched his arm across Greta's shoulders and cuddled her against his chest. "Wake me when we get there."

She glanced up at him. "What? Aren't you going to entertain me with scintillating tales of your boyhood? I keep hearing about the town's baseball team. Surely you've got a few tall tales about that."

"No falsehoods required," he said, resting his head against the back of the seat and closing his eyes. "The Brightfield Bobcats are the best in the league, and we've got the trophy to prove it."

"I bet there's a story there."

"Ask Abigail," George said with a smile. "She'll tell the best version."

Greta relaxed against him. George cuddled her closer and sighed with contentment. She wasn't his wife yet, but she would be. All he had to do was knock down one hurdle at a time. Today would just be another one.

They rode in comfortable silence, each ensconced in his or her thoughts until the train slowed. George woke, but Greta roused first, moving toward the window to look over her hometown.

The conductor passed along the hallway, announcing their arrival. "New Canaan! All off for New Canaan!"

George stretched his arms and yawned. "How's the weather?"

"Sunny," Greta answered over her shoulder. "According to the station clock, we're right on time." She jumped to her feet, retrieved her coat, and slipped it on. "Ready?"

Her eagerness encouraged him. "You bet," he said and got to his feet. They would have to wait for most of the passengers to exit the train and then walk to her father's grocery store but asking Greta to wait would be like telling a child Christmas had been cancelled.

She took his arm once they were on the sidewalk. A cool breeze blew from the east, carrying with it the salty scent of the ocean. Horse-drawn wagons and motorcars clogged the streets of New Canaan, and people scurried in and out of buildings. Most of the buildings had brick facades, but a few had been painted bright colors.

Greta's family business sat on a busy corner. Above its double doors, a black sign with gold lettering featured the store's name — *Horvat's Grocery*. Outside, baskets of fresh fruits and vegetables tempted the public. As Greta moved toward the entrance, a gray-haired, buxom woman stepped out.

"Why Greta!" the woman exclaimed, her mouth dropping to form an oval. "I haven't seen you in...what's it been...a year?"

Greta smiled politely. "Hello, Mrs. Lingelbach. How are you?"

The woman stuttered as she tried to gather her thoughts. "Well, I'm ….where have you been, Greta?"

"I live in Brightfield now." Greta must have wanted to avoid the lady, because she didn't tarry for polite conversation and didn't bother to introduce George. "Is my father in the store? He and Mother are expecting me."

Mrs. Lingelbach closed her mouth and shuffled away from the entrance. "Yes, yes….he's in there."

Greta seized the opportunity to squeeze behind the lady and step through the entrance. She tugged on George's arm so he would follow. "Nice to see you, Mrs. Lingelbach," she called cheerfully.

George tipped his hat to the lady and stepped into the crowded but clean store. The aroma of spices, bread, cheese, and fruit swirled around him. A few customers stood at a long counter on the right, but Greta ignored them and walked straight toward the man at the back of the store.

Wearing a canvas apron that covered him from collar to socks, the man was of medium height and thin build. He'd been stacking boxes of salt on a shelf, but, when he saw Greta, he smiled and returned the cylindrical box to the counter. "There you are," he said, holding out his arms to her.

Greta reached across the counter and took his hands. "Hello, Papa. How are you?"

"Doing all right," he said. "Did you have a good trip?"

"Everything was fine," Greta said. "I brought a guest with me. This is George Mason. He owns the construction company I work for."

He was more than her boss, wasn't he? George brushed off his concern. She couldn't very well introduce him as her fiancé when her parents didn't yet know the truth about her marriage. He smiled and offered his hand. "Good afternoon, Mr. Horvat."

Greta's father narrowed his eyes and inspected George. He shook George's hand, but George could feel the man's hesitation. His daughter had brought a strange man home. Anyone might be reluctant.

"Your mother's upstairs," Mr. Horvat said. "I'll be up as soon as I speak to our new clerk."

Greta twisted her head so she could see the young man standing with the customers. "Who is that?"

"Elmer Dawson's grandson. He started a month ago."

"Wesley? I didn't realize he'd grown so much."

"That's what happens when you leave a place. In your mind, everyone is frozen in time, but they just keep moving right along."

Greta reached into her sack and withdrew a small box. "I have a gift for you, Papa."

Her father took the plain white box and opened it. "Oh, a new pocketknife. Your mother must have told you my old one broke."

"I hope this one will do."

Mr. Horvat opened and closed the larger blade. "It's very nice, Greta. Thank you."

"I'm glad you like it. We'll go upstairs now."

Her father continued to examine the knife as Greta led George behind the counter, through a storeroom packed with crates and baskets, and up a long, narrow staircase. "Smells like Momma is cooking," she said. "Hope you're hungry."

Greta's father had been of small stature, so, when she opened the apartment door, George expected to see a woman who resembled Greta. The woman coming out of the kitchen, however, was more diminutive than her husband.

"Oh Greta!" her mother exclaimed. "Finally!" She pulled Greta into her arms and held her tightly. "You've been gone so long! With nothing but letters." Tears welled in the woman's eyes, and she used the hem of her apron to dry them.

"It's all right, Momma," Greta said tenderly. "The trip from Brightfield is only two hours by train. You could come and visit me."

"No, no," the woman protested. "Your father needs me." Mrs. Horvat stepped back and noticed George standing a few feet behind Greta. "Oh! I didn't know we had a guest."

"Momma, this is George Mason. He owns the construction company I work for."

"I remember," Mrs. Horvat said and offered her hand. "It is nice to meet you."

George had learned to use an extra light touch when he shook hands with a woman, but Greta's mother's hand felt as insubstantial as a bird's skeleton. From his height, he could clearly see her gray hair thinly covered by a black dye. She wore a flower-print dress and a yellow apron and looked as though a capful of wind could blow her over.

Greta reached into her sack and withdrew a purple box. "I brought you a gift, Momma."

"Oh!" Mrs. Horvat exclaimed with delight and removed the lid. "My favorite! You remembered." She removed a white jar, unscrewed the lid, and smelled the lotion inside. "I do so love the scent of orange blossoms. Thank you."

"What are you cooking, Momma?" Greta asked. "It smells wonderful."

"Sarma," she answered. "And crni rižon, of course. Uncle Damir is coming for lunch. He's anxious to see you."

"It will be nice to see him," Greta said. She turned to George. "Momma is preparing a dish that resembles stuffed cabbage and some black risotto. Have you ever had risotto?"

"Never heard of it," George said. "But if it tastes as good as it smells, I'm sure I'll enjoy it."

Mrs. Horvat placed her gift on a side table. "My parents and my husband's parents came from Croatia many years ago. I fix the traditional dishes for special occasions."

George was determined to clean his plate and compliment the food lavishly no matter how it tasted. "I'm looking forward to trying it."

"Do you need help, Momma?" Greta asked.

"No, no. Why don't you make some coffee for our guest? Damir and your father should be here soon."

Mrs. Horvat returned to the kitchen, and Greta lowered her voice so only George could hear. "Are you doing all right?"

George didn't want to add to Greta's concerns, so he did his best to reassure her. "Of course. Your parents seem like very fine people."

"They are. The man who's coming, Damir Marcovic, he's not actually my uncle. He owns the hardware store across the street. He and my parents grew up together."

George placed his hands on her arms. "Everything's fine, Greta. I like your parents, and I'm sure I'll like Mr. Marcovic. You fix the coffee, and I'll sit on that sofa and relax. All right?"

Greta's face colored slightly, and she blew out a breath. "I'm just nervous, that's all. I know what's coming, and I know how my mother will react, and….well, I'm dreading it."

George squeezed her arms gently. "I'm right here, Greta. I'm not going anywhere. We'll face this together, and we'll get through this together."

Greta turned her head to check on her mother's location. Seeing she was safely occupied in the kitchen, Greta gave him a one-arm hug before joining her mother.

George settled into the plain, brown sofa and rested his left ankle on his right knee. The parlor was small, but the wide windows that overlooked the busy street allowed ample light to enter the room. Mrs. Horvat had added all sorts of homey touches - flowered curtains and small area rugs - giving the room a comfortable and cozy character.

The sound of heavy footsteps on the stairs signaled an impending arrival. In anticipation of Greta's father, George stood. Mr. Horvat entered first, followed closely by something George rarely saw — a man equal to his height and breadth. Greta's father introduced the man. "George, this is Damir Marcovic, longtime friend of the family."

George gazed into Mr. Marcovic's eyes and felt his heart skip a beat. Damir's eyes were exactly the same as Greta's. She must have gotten her height from him, the best friend who'd remained close to the Horvats for many years. Damir had the same straight nose and well-formed lips as Greta, and his hair color was identical. Surely, he was Greta's real father.

George let out the breath he'd been unconsciously holding and shook Damir's hand. No wonder Greta had been troubled by gossip her whole life. Everyone in town had probably realized the truth. For Mr. and Mrs. Horvath to raise a child so unlike them must have been like a cuckoo in the nest.

He was relieved when Mrs. Horvat called them to the table, saving him from awkward small talk with Damir. Did Mr. Horvat know? The resemblance between Damir and Greta was unmistakable, and George wondered if Mr. Horvat had known before he married or had forgiven his wife's infidelity and loved her child as his own? Either way, it had been a virtuous act of love and honor, and George's esteem for the man rose.

Once they were all seated around the rectangular table, Mr. Horvat said a brief blessing over the food, and the dishes were passed. Damir loaded his plate with the aromatic food. "Marta is the only person I know who can cook like my mother," he said, practically smacking his lips. "You're in for a treat today, George."

"Oh, stop it." Greta's mother said with a shake of her head. "You know there are many ladies at church who make the same dishes."

"I'm sure everything is delicious," George said, allowing Greta to spoon the meat dish onto his plate.

"And the black risotto?" Damir continued. "When you eat it, you get a surprise."

George raised an eyebrow toward Greta. "Nothing bad," she promised with a shake of the head. "You'll see."

Damir laughed loudly and scooped the food into his mouth. "Wonderful, Marta. I don't care what you say, you're the best!"

Mr. Horvat smiled across the table at his blushing wife.

George's curiosity wouldn't be satisfied on this trip, but Greta's true parentage could explain why Mr. Horvat had left the child-rearing responsibilities to his wife.

"Tell us about the doctor you work with," her father said.

Greta spoke at length about Benjamin's clinic. She described some of the cases he'd treated, how hard he worked, and how Abigail had become a special friend. George rarely thought of Benjamin in that way. To him, Benjamin was his sister's husband, the lead pitcher on the baseball team, and the town doctor. "In fact," she concluded, "Abigail is George's sister."

"Well, well," Damir said around a mouthful of food. "Big family in a small town, eh? What do you do for a living, George?"

George leaned back in his chair. "I just opened my own construction business. At the moment, I'm working on a contract for ten houses."

"Construction," Mr. Horvat said, "is one of those businesses that's always needed. Like groceries. People need to eat, and people need places to live."

"I hope you'll come to Brightfield and see what George is building," Greta said. "It's a whole new style of house. Very modern and very beautiful."

"Can't get away from the store," Mr. Horvat said. "You know that."

"Not even on a Sunday?" Greta asked. "You could take the morning train and come back in the evening."

"I don't know," her father said with a shake of his head.

Greta looked down at her plate in silence. Beneath the table, George slid his hand over hers. Her father probably hadn't meant his comment to sound like a rejection.

At his touch, a small smile crossed her lips, and Greta lifted her head. "Looks like everyone is finished, Momma. Shall I bring in the coffee?"

"Oh yes," her mother said, getting to her feet. "And I'll bring the cake."

"The food was delicious," George said. "But I didn't notice any surprises."

The others laughed softly. "Look," Greta said. She smiled widely and stuck out the end of her tongue.

Greta's lips and tongue were stained black. "Oh!" George said with a laugh. "I suppose mine are the same?"

"We all have black tongues!" Damir said and showed his tongue as proof. "The black risotto is made with squid ink!"

"That's a first for me," George said. "But it tasted good nonetheless."

Damir raised his voice to be heard in the kitchen. "What kind of cake, Marta? Kolač?"

"Of course," answered Mrs. Horvat's faint voice.

"Apple cake," Greta explained. "It's very good." She loaded her arms with empty plates and disappeared through the kitchen door.

Mr. Horvat cleared his throat. "George, while the ladies are gone, tell me why you've come today."

George liked Mr. Horvat more and more. He'd always admired a person who got straight to the point. "Greta and I have something to discuss with you and her mother." He glanced at Damir. "Something private."

"Yeah, yeah," Damir said with a scowl. "I got the message. After the cake I will go. But you should know one thing. I might be in New Canaan, and you might be in Brightfield, but if I hear about Greta being hurt, I can get on a train and beat your head so far into the ground you'll look like an ostrich."

George had to bite his cheek not to laugh. Damir might match George's size, but Damir was at least twenty years older. George had no doubt who would win a fistfight. George leveled his gaze at the older man. "You have nothing to worry about."

The expression on Damir's face showed a definite lack of conviction. "She's a married woman. You know that, right?"

"I know about her marriage," George answered, intent on keeping his cards close to his chest.

Damir scowled, but he let the matter go. George glanced at Greta's father. How odd Damir should protect Greta instead of him. Mr. Horvat surely knew the truth about his daughter's conception. He, his wife, and his friend had lived with the secret for decades. George wasn't about to disclose his suspicions.

The ladies returned with the dessert, and the convivial mood returned. True to his word, Damir claimed a need to return to his store, said his farewells, and left with a strongly gripped handshake and a threatening glare for George.

CHAPTER TWELVE

Greta sat at the table and watched the spring breeze flutter the faded curtains. The polite conversation had ended, and it was time to tell her parents about Emile Franklin's deceit and George's sincerity. Deep inside her body, a trembling apprehension began. Her story ended well, she reminded herself. But before she got to the ending, she'd have to pass through a gauntlet of disapproval.

Greta's mother stood and reached for the dirty dishes. "Wait, Momma. I'll take care of it. For now, I have something I need to tell you and Papa."

Her mother closed her eyes, sighed, and fell back into her chair.

"I thought as much. What's happened now?"

The defeated tone in her mother's voice twisted Greta's heart. She'd heard it so often. "A few weeks ago, a woman named Millie Franklin found me in Brightfield."

"Someone in Emile's family?" her mother asked.

Despite her discomfort, Greta had to smile. "You could say that," she answered. She took a deep breath and related the story she'd rehearsed. She told every detail, every emotion, every surprise, and every outrage of what had happened.

Her mother and father listened quietly, their faces clearly showing their disdain. When Greta finally reached the end, they sat in silence, her father staring sightlessly through the open window, and her mother covering her face with her hand.

"I should have known," her father said at last. "He was a salesman, after all, and he sold himself as well as he sold products from Washburn Mills."

"What I never understood," her mother added, "is why you accepted his proposal in the first place. You knew I needed you here, and you knew he would take you away, but you married that fool anyway."

Greta wanted to reach out her hand in supplication but feared her mother would reject it. "I thought he would be my only chance," she said in a timid, little girl voice. "I want to have a husband and children of my own, Momma. Why shouldn't I have what every other woman has? And, after so many years of being snubbed by the boys and men around here, I thought he was my only chance."

Her mother shook her head slowly from side-to-side. "Marriage and motherhood aren't what you think. It's no happy ever after."

Greta glanced at her father. Surely, he would react to such an assertion. But his gaze never left the open window.

George leaned forward and spoke for the first time since Greta had started her story. "When I discovered Greta was not a married woman, I made it clear I was interested in courting her. As you know, I have my own business, and I'm more than capable of providing for a wife and children. I came today so you could meet me."

A small sound of distress came from her mother. "Just when I hoped you'd come home," she whispered.

Greta faced her mother. "Momma, I love you very much. I would never abandon you if you needed me. But you're asking me to sacrifice all my future happiness."

Her mother's expression turned from piteous to harsh. "You want to talk about sacrifice? I'll tell you about sacrifice. Do you think I dreamed of being a grocer's wife? Do you think I hoped to live in a four-room apartment above a store?"

Greta had hoped to avoid this reaction. Whenever she'd tried to explain herself in the past, her mother had usually turned it into a story of her own hardship. She looked down at her empty plate and blinked back her tears.

George slid his arm around her shoulders and leaned toward her mother. "Greta and I hope to have a wedding in Brightfield. We would like both of you to be there. We haven't set a date, but we'll be sure to give you plenty of notice so you can make arrangements for your store. And, if it helps, I give you my word that Greta and I will gladly help you or her father in any way we can if the need arises in the future."

Her father made a dismissive sound low in his throat. "Not exactly asking permission, are you?"

George turned toward him and answered in a calm tone. "No, sir. But I am asking for your blessing."

Greta took a deep breath, inhaling George's strength and certainty. Her parents held no power over him. Her mother couldn't drown him with guilt.

Greta's father stood. "I'm going back downstairs. Come say goodbye before you leave, Greta."

Greta kept her gaze on the table. "Of course, Papa." She heard the door open and close. Her mother sniffed loudly and stood. A few moments later, she heard her mother's bedroom door close. Greta dropped her head to the table and let her tears fall.

George placed a calming hand on her tremulous shoulders. "It could have been worse," he said in a gentle voice.

Greta winced to imagine a worse scenario. She'd wanted her parents to rejoice at her freedom from Emile and her future with George, but she'd disappointed them. It seemed they were always disappointed in her. Greta stood, reached for the empty plates, and carried them into the kitchen. George followed, carrying his own load of dishes. At the sink, he offered her his clean handkerchief.

Greta dried her eyes. "It was easier with you here. Thank you for coming."

"Think I'd let you enter the lion's cage by yourself?"

Greta smiled in spite of her tears. "After I clean the kitchen, I'll speak to my mother. Then, I'll tell Papa goodbye, and we can leave."

"Train doesn't leave for a few hours. Is there someone else you'd like to see before we leave?"

"Not really. We can take a walk if you'd like. Might be good to stretch our legs before we ride back."

George crossed his arms and leaned against the cabinet. "What have your parents told you about that family friend, the one you call Uncle Damir?"

Greta's eyebrows drew together as she considered his unexpected question. "Nothing special. My grandparents and his parents knew each other in Croatia. They came to the United States on the same ship and traveled to New Canaan because there was already a community of Croatian immigrants here. My parents and Damir were born in New Canaan, and they grew up together. That's really all I know. What makes you ask about him?"

"Because I think your parents have been keeping a secret from you. Haven't you noticed that you don't look like either your mother or your father?"

Why was George asking her about this? "Of course I have. I used to wonder if I was adopted, but my birth certificate has my mother's and father's names."

A note of caution entered George's voice. "You don't look like your parents, but you do resemble Uncle Damir. I don't know the specifics, but I believe *he's* your father."

Greta's thoughts froze. What had George said? Uncle Damir and her mother? Memories streamed through her mind. Damir at her birthday dinners, Damir at graduation, Damir at all the important moments of her life. It was possible. Unthinkable, but possible. Poor Papa. "Do you think ...." Greta swallowed and tried again. "Do you think my father knows?"

George stroked her back tenderly. "It would explain why he kept his distance while you were growing up."

It was more than possible for Damir to be her real father, she realized. It was probable. "Papa wasn't very involved, but he loves me."

"I agree." George's soft voice soothed her anxiety. "But you're not the only one in your family who has a secret. You've told me how difficult it was for you to grow up with people talking about you, and you concluded they were criticizing your appearance. But I think it's more likely those gossips were talking about your mother and Uncle Damir. Don't feel bad about keeping information from your parents. They kept something much more important from you."

Greta crossed her arms and lowered her head. She wasn't surprised her parents had never told her. She'd been too young to understand. She walked away from George and moved to the window. The busy street below faded from view as she considered the gossip she'd overheard in her father's store. Could those women have been talking about Damir?

George seemed to sense she needed to be apart from him, because he stayed in the kitchen. "You know," he began, "I can only imagine what it would be like to have people talk behind my back. I've never had to face the kind of embarrassment you've described. If it were possible, I'd shoulder all your worries for you, but it's not necessary. You've already proven you can slay dragons."

All of Greta's concerns faded as George's words sank into her heart. He didn't understand, but he sympathized, nonetheless. The question of her true paternity wasn't as important as the man who'd stood by her side as she'd battled her embarrassment.

Greta turned from the window and approached him slowly. "As long as I live, I'm never going to forget today. You've really seen me, George, and you love me anyway."

He wrapped his arms around her in a gentle embrace and kissed her forehead. Greta breathed out a heavy sigh as she relaxed in his arms. "I love you, George Mason."

He laughed softly and tightened his hold. "Right back at you, Greta Horvat."

"Oh, that's right!" she said, stepping out of his embrace. "Since I was never married, I suppose my name isn't Franklin."

"You can call yourself Greta Goldfish for all I care. As long as you're Greta Mason someday."

"Greta Goldfish sounds like a mermaid's name. Hello, I'm Greta Goldfish, and I live in the Caribbean Sea. I spend my day riding seahorses and eating oysters."

"And do you write with squid ink?" George asked, joining in her fun.

"No, I use squid ink to brush my teeth." She smiled broadly, opening her mouth to show the full effect of black risotto.

"I think you should fix that dish for my family," George said.

"I'd love to play a trick on my brothers."

"Hard to get fresh squid in Brightfield," Greta replied.

"I guess so," George agreed. "Still...it would be fun, wouldn't it?"

Greta wrapped her arms around his neck and stood on tiptoe to place her cheek on his. "Thank you for today. Every time I considered not telling my parents, there you were, encouraging me and silently reminding me my future doesn't have to be like my past. I can't wait to marry you."

George kissed her forehead. Greta emitted a small sound, a cross between a sigh and a moan. She offered her mouth, and he took his time kissing her.

"Keep kissing me like that," Greta whispered, "and I'll be asking for an early wedding date."

"You won't get an argument from me." George stroked her hair and kissed her again.

She still had to reassure her mother and speak to her father, but Greta couldn't keep anything in her brain except the feel of George's lips and the exhilaration of his embrace. When she was in his arms, she felt comfort and passion. When the time was right, she would give herself to George with all her heart.

CHAPTER THIRTEEN

Greta followed Abigail into Hildy's favorite dress shop the same way she would have entered a swamp. She wasn't expecting alligators and snakes, but, in her experience, the bites of critical salesgirls and fault-finding seamstresses could be almost as bad.

The owner had decorated her shop with feminine touches. Pastel pink draperies framed the windows and vases of fresh flowers had been placed on every empty surface. Lacy scarves and flowered hats hung from the walls, and perfume bottles enticed shoppers to experiment with the new scent.

Hildy was immediately greeted by a stylishly dressed middle-aged woman with auburn hair. "Oh, Mrs. Mason, how nice to see you again."

Hildy smiled politely. "Thank you, Beatrice. Let me introduce my guests. This is my sister-in-law, Abigail Connor."

"What a beauty!" the shopkeeper exclaimed. "With that blonde hair and those blue eyes, all the pastels will suit you. We have some beautiful things for spring."

Abigail blushed and looked at Hildy who quickly came to her rescue. "Don't throw everything at her at once, Beatrice "

The shopkeeper laughed softly. "Don't worry, Miss Abigail. Just relax and let me spoil you."

"My other guest," Hildy said, turning to Greta, "is my future sister-in-law. Allow me to introduce Greta Franklin."

Beatrice turned and looked up at Greta. "Oh, Miss Greta, how wonderfully tall you are."

Greta blinked in disbelief. Her height had been commented on all her life, but it had never been described as wonderful.

"But your hat," the shopkeeper continued, "is all wrong. I'm going to show you the right hat for that beautiful face."

Greta touched her head self-consciously. She'd purchased a brown wool cloche with a small brim for everyday wear. What could be wrong with it?

The shopkeeper motioned to a nearby salesgirl. "Get the private salon ready for our special guests."

"Yes ma'am," the girl said before disappearing through a curtained exit.

"Are you looking for anything special?" Beatrice asked the three of them. "Maybe a wedding dress?"

Greta's spirits surged at the mention of a wedding dress but affording one in this store would undoubtedly go against her thrifty nature. "Oh, I don't know…."

"It never hurts to look," Hildy said. "You may find the perfect dress here or you may simply get an idea of what you like."

"We're preparing a few light refreshments for you," the shopkeeper said. "Come and make yourselves comfortable in our private room. We'll bring a selection of clothing for you to consider."

Beatrice led Greta and the others through a curtained entrance to a room furnished with plush chairs upholstered in flowered fabric. A silver teapot and coffee pot waited on a side table beside china cups. "Make yourselves comfortable, ladies," Beatrice said, "but Miss Greta, please sit here in front of the mirror."

Greta glanced at Hildy and Abigail. They both encouraged her with smiles and nods, so Greta laid her purse on one of the chairs and moved to the bench Beatrice had indicated.

"Now," said Beatrice, removing Greta's hat, "let me show you the best hat for the shape of your face."

In the mirror, Greta saw the shop owner beckon to someone, and a salesgirl appeared carrying two hats.

Beatrice took a black hat from the girl and set it on Greta's head. "Look how this one softens your face."

It was the largest hat Greta had ever seen. The ample brim was at least three inches wide, and white silk roses surrounded the crown.

"How lovely," Hildy gushed.

Abigail moved next to Greta. "It really makes a difference."

Greta put a hand on each side of the wide brim. "How do I make it through a doorway with this thing on?" Greta asked.

"It's not as hard as you think," Hildy said with a laugh. "That's my favorite style. The bigger, the better."

"A wide brim narrows the face," Beatrice explained. She took the second hat from the salesgirl. "If you're not comfortable with it, you might consider this modified beret."

Beatrice removed the large-brimmed hat and set the second hat on Greta's head. "Now, when you choose a smaller hat, consider angling it to one side."

Abigail bent at the waist so that her head was level with Greta's. "I can't believe such a little thing makes such a big difference."

Greta studied her reflection. The shop owner certainly knew her business. She'd been in the store for less than half an hour and was already estimating the cost of two hats.

"What about me?" Abigail said, removing her wide-brimmed straw hat. "Which hat style suits me?"

Greta relinquished her seat on the bench to Abigail.

"Come sit by me," Hildy said, pointing to an empty chair. "I poured you some coffee."

Greta sat in one of the chairs and sipped her coffee. Considering the shopkeeper's behavior, Hildy must shop here often. Greta had never been treated so well by a merchant.

Finished with the hats, Abigail joined them. "I feel like a princess in this store. Are those sandwiches?" She went to the side table and filled a plate with finger sandwiches and cookies. She returned and offered the treats to Greta. "Have you and George met with Reverend Hixson yet?"

"Tomorrow," Greta answered, taking a sandwich.

Hildy chose several cookies. "Sometimes I think Reverend Hixson is still living in the nineteenth century. I hope everything goes well for you."

"I'm a little nervous," Greta said. "I'm afraid Reverend Hixson will judge me harshly. I didn't use very good judgment when I married Emile, and I went against my parents' wishes."

Hildy crossed her arms in front of her chest. "The only people who would blame you instead of your so-called husband are the mean, stupid ones."

Abigail burst into laughter. "Oh Hildy! Just when I think you never say a mean thing about anyone, you come out with something like that."

"Well, it's true, isn't it?" Hildy asserted. "Our Greta married someone who presented himself as an honorable, hard-working man, only to find out he was a wolf in sheep's clothing."

"I appreciate your kind words, but I certainly feel stupid sometimes," Greta admitted. "I should have known better."

"It almost happened to me," Hildy said, "and I'm not stupid."

Greta couldn't believe what she'd heard. Hildy Campbell Mason, successful businesswoman, paragon of style and grace, had once been duped?

"You're right," Abigail said. "It's a lot like that confidence man. Tell Greta what happened."

Hildy turned her gaze toward Greta. "My father always told me I had to marry someone who had their own fortune. He thought it was the only way I could be sure a fortune hunter wouldn't take advantage of me."

"Is that why you married Andrew?" Greta asked.

"Heavens no!" Hildy answered. "I am over-the-moon in love with my husband, but I almost rejected him because he had no money. I was very close to accepting a proposal from a Wall Street investor when I discovered he was after my money."

"It was a close call," Abigail added. "Andrew was ready to give up on Hildy, but he was the one who discovered the truth."

Hildy stood and reached for the coffee pot. "Sometimes girls believe things that simply aren't true. Our mothers tell us things that they believe to be accurate but aren't. Our friends and teachers and even our ministers tell us the way we should be in the world without ever considering what's best for us."

"Like women's suffrage," Abigail said. "Reverend Hixson thinks it's a dangerous idea that will lead to —"

"Total dissolution of the home," Hildy finished. "If he says that one more time, I'm going to stand up in the middle of the service and tell him what I think."

"I can't wait to see that!" Abigail crowed.

A question popped into Greta's mind. "Did the two of you get married in our church?"

"I did," answered Abigail. "And Reverend Hixson performed the ceremony."

"Same for me," said Hildy. "But Greta, that doesn't mean you have to do the same."

"I was just wondering...do you think it's important to George? I mean, he grew up in that church."

Abigail shrugged. "I'm not sure. My big brother has never been the sentimental type."

"Did you have your heart set on a church wedding, Greta?" Hildy asked.

"Not really. I'd like to have a minister, but a church isn't that important."

"Well, my house is always available," Hildy volunteered. "You could use the main rooms or the garden."

"Ooh," crooned Abigail. "The garden. Hildy's garden in spring is a sight to behold."

"That sounds lovely," Greta said, "but I've been thinking about the orchard."

"The orchard!" Abigail said. "I never considered that. It's so lovely this time of year. Hildy, we could set up tables of food and maybe a flower arch and we could get chairs or benches for the guests."

"Hold on!" Greta said between laughs. "You're organizing it before George and I have time to plan."

"Oh," enthused Abigail, "it would be so much fun!"

"But what if it rains?" asked Hildy.

"Maybe we could rig up some kind of tent," suggested Abigail.

Greta held out her hand, palm out. "Stop! I'm begging you, stop!"

Their laughter rang through the cozy room. Greta took several deep breaths. She couldn't remember the last time she'd laughed so much. If she left it up to them, Greta was certain she could sleep for a week and every detail of her wedding would be handled when she awoke. "I'd prefer you wait until I speak to George."

Abigail cupped her hand around her mouth as though she were telling a secret. "I think Greta's trying to tell us something," Abigail said in a stage whisper.

Hildy copied Abigail's gesture. "I think she wants us to butt out."

"All right, you two," Greta said in mock annoyance. "Is it time I confess how happy I am to be part of this family? Must I admit how lovely it is to be with two of my favorite people in the world?"

"Ohhh…." Abigail and Hildy crooned as they moved to embrace Greta simultaneously.

"I wish Helen had come," Greta said past the lump in her throat. "Then everything would be perfect."

"I agree," Hildy said, touching a small handkerchief to her eyes. "Perhaps we can convince her to accompany us next time."

"I'm not sure," Abigail said with a loud sniff. "The only shopping she does is from the Sears Roebuck catalog."

The shop owner returned with two salesgirls wheeling a rack of dresses. "Here we are, ladies. I've selected something for each of you that will be perfect for spring."

Greta's heart made a peculiar lurch when she noticed four white dresses on the rack. Would she find her wedding dress today? Since her mother couldn't be with her, the next best thing would be her new friends.

Hildy removed one of the white dresses and studied it. "Try this one, Greta. It's perfect for your shape."

Abigail chose another dress. "And this one. I have a dress that's almost the same. The wide sash minimizes my waistline."

Greta waited for their laughter or an insult wrapped inside a teasing comment, but there was no ridicule behind their words. She took both dresses and stepped behind the dressing screen.

George had brought so many good things into her life, including the two women with her. In order to marry Emile, she had shoved her misgivings and insecurities deep within herself. But things would be different this time. She was no longer the timid girl who waited for the world to give its permission to be herself.

***

George steered his truck too quickly around the curve leading to the church, but he didn't bother to slow down. He was late to meet with Reverend Hixson. After prompting Greta to make the appointment every day for a week, arriving late would not be a good way to start.

As the church came into view, he saw Greta standing near the entrance. Her expression signaled anxiety, but he didn't know if that was caused by his tardiness or her disinclination to speak to the minister. Either way, they'd be sitting across from their pastor in a few moments.

George got out of the truck, hurried to Greta's side, and gave her a one-arm hug. "Sorry to make you wait."

"You forget," she said with a warm smile. "I'm probably the one person who knows how busy you are. Is everything all right at the site?"

"Everything is under control." George took her arm and led her around the side of the building where Reverend Hixson's office was located. "After our meeting, I'll drive you home and then return to finish the day."

A small white wooden sign with black letters labeled the office door. Greta lifted her hand to knock, then lowered it and looked at George. "Reverend Hixson is a widower, right?"

"That's right," George said. "His wife died two, maybe three years ago. Why do you ask?"

"I was just wondering how sympathetic he might be to our predicament. Well, *my* predicament."

"He's our minister," George said. "Isn't it his job to be sympathetic?"

Greta didn't seem to be convinced, but she knocked softly on the office door. "Come on in!" answered Reverend Hixson's booming voice.

"Good afternoon, Reverend," Greta said as she stepped into the small room.

Their pastor was invariably cheerful. "Hello there! Nice to see you." Reverend Hixson stood and shook George's hand. Then he indicated they should seat themselves in the two wooden chairs facing his desk. "Isn't this a beautiful day? I do love the spring weather." George waited for Greta to settle into her chair and then sat beside her.

Reverend Hixson's smile never faltered. "How's your family, George?"

"Everyone's fine, Reverend."

"I saw Abigail and your mother at the Ladies' Circle meeting. They're looking well and working hard on the children's party."

George wasn't sure how he was supposed to respond. He knew nothing about his mother's activities and even less about the children's party.

"Now then," the minister said, "what did you want to see me about?"

Anxiety shadowed Greta's eyes, so George decided to speak for both of them. "Well, Reverend, the thing is, Greta and I would like to be married."

A frown of confusion darkened the pastor's face. He looked at Greta. "Aren't you already married, Mrs. Franklin?"

"I thought I was," she answered with a tremble in her voice. "But I recently discovered my so-called husband married me without ending his first marriage."

Reverend Hixson rested his elbows on his desk and leaned closer to them. He was all-business now. "Oh my. This sounds quite serious."

Greta glanced at George, silently asking him to continue. George shifted in his chair and retold the events of the last month. He reported them chronologically, filling in the minister on the important points, answering whatever questions the clergyman posed, and ending with their recent trip to New Canaan. "So you see," he concluded, "the way is finally clear for us to be married, and we'd like to proceed."

Reverend Hixson leaned back in his chair and rubbed his cheek with the palm of his hand. "What a story. I had no idea."

George waited for his minister to process the information. It was a lot to take in. A fraudulent marriage, an honorable woman who'd been dishonored by a scoundrel, and a man and woman who wanted to put it all behind them. After several long minutes, Reverend Hixson looked at them and tapped his desk. "Well, I only see one thing standing in your way."

"What's that?" George asked cautiously.

Reverend Hixson pointed to Greta. "You're going to need to inform the congregation."

George felt more than heard Greta's soft gasp. "Me?"

"Definitely," the minister answered. "You presented yourself to this church as a married woman. We accepted you into our fellowship as a married woman. You and George cannot simply announce your upcoming nuptials without an explanation."

"How...what…?" Greta's uneasiness was increasing.

"What do you expect Greta to do?" George asked.

"At the end of every service, just before the benediction, I have an altar call. That would be a good time for Mrs. Franklin to explain her situation to the congregation."

"Oh no," Greta said, shaking her head. "From the first day I visited this church, I've been subjected to pointed questions about where my husband was and when he might be home. Some people suspected I'd made him up. Now you expect me to tell everyone my secrets?"

Greta's distress flowed straight into George's heart. He'd never really thought about how hard it had been for her. "Reverend, are you saying Greta needs to address the congregation or that it needs to be done? Because I —"

Reverend Hixson held up a hand to cut him off. "It needs to be Greta. She joined this church as a married woman. She made friends based on that understanding. If you and she were to marry without clarifying matters, she'd be considered a liar or a fraud. The Mason family is one of the bedrock families of this congregation. Adding Greta would defame your family's name."

The first sparks of anger kindled in George's gut. Had he heard his minister correctly? "Reverend, Greta could never defame my family's name."

"Oh, I know the Masons are one of Brightfield's finest families, but they are not immune to the effect of adding a woman with Greta's past."

George sat forward on his chair. "No, Reverend Hixson. I'm not saying my family is immune. I'm saying Greta is an honorable woman. She did nothing wrong. She was tricked by an unprincipled man, but *she* did nothing wrong."

Reverend Hixson's voice took on the tone of an adult talking to a child. "Well, George, of course you think that way. You're obviously quite fond of Greta. But I have to think about the whole congregation and how this type of revelation will affect them. A married woman with an absentee husband confesses she was never really married? Surely you can see how that will sow seeds of discontent among the church."

George's skin prickled as his anger rose. "I hope I'm hearing you wrong, Reverend. In Greta's mind, she was legally married. Her so-called husband abandoned her, but she didn't do anything to cause it. She was hoodwinked because she believed what she'd been told. Her only sin was trusting the wrong man."

"Exactly," the minister agreed. "I can't imagine Greta's parents condoned her marriage to such a man. A young woman should rely on her parents to find a good husband for her. Then, after a year of courting, a marriage is arranged. From what you told me, Mrs. Franklin didn't do any of those things. Her lack of good sense means she must pay the consequences. Addressing the members of the church is just one of those consequences."

Greta lowered her head and covered her face with her hands, and George's temper went from simmer to full boil. He'd never imagined his own minister could be so indifferent to Greta's situation. He shot to his feet and glared at the minister. Any other man would feel the sting of George's temper, but since he was a clergyman, George fought his first instinct. He turned to Greta. "We're leaving."

CHAPTER FOURTEEN

Greta didn't hesitate. Without saying a word, she got to her feet and strode out of the office. George turned to say one last thing to his minister, but finding nothing but harsh words on his tongue, he put on his hat and followed Greta outside.

She was pacing in front of his truck, her arms crossed tightly against her chest. As he approached, she turned her back.

"He was wrong to talk to you that way," George offered.

She did not respond. George's anger had begun to dissipate, but Greta's emotions were obviously still running high.

"I'll talk to him again," George promised. "Later. When I don't want to punch him in the nose."

"Talking to him won't do any good."

"Why do you say that?"

"Didn't you hear him? He wants me to face the people in this church and confess my sins. And sweetheart, I won't do it."

"Greta, you never did anything wrong."

"Oh yes, I did. Didn't you hear him? I misrepresented myself. I disobeyed my parents and didn't use good judgment. According to Reverend Hixson, you and I should court for a year before we get married."

"There's no way I'm waiting a whole year. Besides, Andrew got married in this church, and he didn't court Hildy for a year."

"Well, apparently Reverend Hixson has different standards for different people. But you may as well forget about getting married in that church. I'm not good enough."

George had limited experience dealing with angry women. His mother had been angry at him over the years, but it had always been well-deserved. His sister could also build up quite a head of steam whenever he failed to notice her frustration. But Greta's anger seemed to come from a deep taproot of outrage.

He wanted to comfort her, but the straight set of her shoulders and the rigid posture of her spine didn't invite gentle caresses. He wanted to make everything right, but his best-laid plans for the minister had shattered, and he wasn't sure where to step next. "Greta?"

She turned to look at him. Instead of anger flashing in her eyes, he saw the emptiness of resignation. He decided to stick to the bottom line. "I want to marry you. I want to have a family with you. I want you to be at my side and work with me toward achieving our dreams. And I don't care if I have to marry you on a dirt road in the middle of nowhere, I will do it."

The smallest of smiles teased her lips. "There are lots of ministers."

"Exactly."

"And there are lots of churches."

"There sure are."

"So, a dirt road in the middle of nowhere probably isn't our only choice."

George reached her in one step, pulled her into his arms, and kissed her. She wasn't giving up and he never would. When he ended the kiss, he nestled her head against his shoulder. "Where would you like to get married?"

She gave a small shrug. "Your parents' house? Or the orchard? We're not required to have Reverend Hixson marry us in the sanctuary."

"That's good because right now I'm about two inches away from breaking his jaw."

"George, you wouldn't."

"No, I wouldn't. But that doesn't lower my desire to do it."

Greta tightened her hold on him. "I love the way you stood up for me. You helped me stand up to my parents, and today you stood up to our minister."

Didn't Greta know he'd do anything for her? She was braver than she knew and didn't need him to fight her battles, but George wanted to be with her anyway. He'd find a way around Reverend Hixson and his outlandish condition.

***

George stared out the window of the warehouse office and sighed loudly. Two straight days of rain had stopped almost all the work at the building site. The workmen didn't get paid when they didn't work, but George wouldn't let anyone risk injury on wet roofs or wet scaffolds. The interior painters had finished everything the day before, and only a few carpenters were installing trim, baseboards, and built-in shelving.

Greta sat in her own desk directly across from George. She had one pencil pushed into the bun at the back of her head and another in her hand. A frown of concentration wrinkled her forehead as she worked on two open ledgers. She had arrived wearing a new blue dress and a wide-brimmed blue hat with white flowers. George had complimented her on the new outfit, and she had turned to show off how the style flattered her figure. He could appreciate good design whether it was for a building or a dress, but what impressed him more was the increased self-confidence she exhibited. Whenever he'd complimented her appearance before, she'd rolled her eyes or ducked her head. This time, she'd twirled for him like star ballerina.

Greta turned a page in each ledger and pursed her lips in concentration. What would happen, George wondered, if he got on all fours and crawled across his desk to hers. A few kisses would probably change that frown to a smile. Or should he ease around her back and blow on her ear? Would she jump when startled or laugh at his antics?

As though reading his devilish thoughts, she looked up from her work and smiled. "I thought Henry was coming by."

George removed his pocket watch. "He said three o'clock. Guess he's on his way." Greta turned another page in one of the ledgers and returned her attention to the column of numbers. George leaned forward and rested his arms on his desk. "I've been wanting to talk to you about where we're going to live after we get married."

Greta put down her pencil and gave him her full attention. "I don't think you'd like the boarding house."

"No, I don't believe I would. I'd prefer privacy when I'm alone with my wife in our bedroom."

Greta covered her reddening face with her hand. "George!"

He smiled at her discomfort. "I haven't done more than kiss you, but that doesn't mean I haven't been thinking about our wedding night."

Greta dropped her head into the open ledger. "You're determined to embarrass me, aren't you?"

"You make it so easy."

"What's your idea about where to live?" she said, her face still resting atop the ledger.

"That depends on the date of the wedding. My crew can put up the shell of a house in about three weeks. The roof, siding, and everything else takes at least two weeks more. My dad has always said he'd give each of his children two acres to live on when they were ready to build their own houses, so, unless you object, we could build there."

Greta raised her head. "Next to your parents?"

"Anywhere on the farm. We could even live near the orchard if you'd like."

"Is living out there all right with you?"

"Sure. We'd have plenty of privacy, and no one would be able to hear what goes on in our bedroom." He laughed as her face dropped into the open ledger again.

"What do you think about the last Saturday in May?" George asked. "That'll give me time to get our new house in a livable condition. You might have to put up with workmen and construction mess for a few weeks, but we'd have a roof over our heads and a working kitchen and bathroom."

Greta straightened in her chair and flipped the pages of her desk calendar. "That's four weeks from now."

"I know you want to do everything the traditional way. Is the end of May too soon?"

"No, I can be ready by then. What do you think about having the ceremony in the orchard?"

"I don't have any objections, but the blossoms aren't there anymore."

A slow smile crept over Greta's mouth. "It's a special place. It's where you first kissed me."

George's heart warmed at the memory. "I haven't forgotten. Want me to reenact the moment for you?"

Greta's cheeks pinkened. "I like your kisses, but I don't want Henry to walk in on us. I also like privacy."

"Ah-ha! You've been thinking about our wedding night too, haven't you?"

Greta covered her face with her hands. "I'll never tell!"

George couldn't remember the last time he'd been so happy. "So, I'll start preparing a building site near the orchard, and you pick the house design you like best." George passed her the same five drawings Hildy had given him several months earlier. "What do you need me to do for the wedding ceremony?"

Greta slipped the drawings under the ledger books. "Nothing I can think of. Hildy and Abigail liked the idea of having the ceremony in the orchard, so I wouldn't be surprised if those two have the whole thing planned."

"You've been talking to them about the wedding?"

"When we went shopping."

"I told Mom about the things Reverend Hixson said to you. She agreed you should tell the congregation about your first marriage."

Greta stared at him and spoke with steel in her voice. "If you think I'm willing to stand up in front of everybody and tell them about Emile, you can just forget about a wedding."

George's heart skipped a beat. Greta was still angry. Surely that's why she'd made such a threat. "Mom also said he was wrong to criticize you."

"Criticism is —"

"Sorry to make you wait," Henry said as he hurried through the office door.

Greta closed her mouth and leaned back in her seat.

"Now," Henry said, pulling a wooden chair up to George's desk, "what more do we need to do for that hospital bid?"

"It's finished," Greta answered, reaching for a leather portfolio.

George kept his eye on Greta as she showed Henry how she had organized the different sections of their bid. He had a date for the wedding, and a location for their house, but the matter of who would perform the wedding was far from over. Their minister had said hurtful things, but even if a different minister performed the ceremony, he and Greta would be sitting in Reverend Hixson's sanctuary every Sunday morning. He needed a peacemaker, someone who could make his minister understand and his fiancee forgive.

If only he knew who to ask.

CHAPTER FIFTEEN

Greta had not forgotten Reverend Hixson's unreasonable condition for conducting her wedding ceremony. As she tidied Dr. Connor's office the next afternoon, she mentally practiced what she'd like to say to her minister. In her calmer moments, she could almost understand the necessity of explaining her situation to the congregation, but surely there was a way to do it without confessing her mistakes to everyone.

She would never agree to a one year courtship. Perhaps she'd married Emile for the wrong reasons, but she'd never suspected his dishonesty. He'd paid attention to her and had told her what she'd always wanted to hear. No wonder she'd been so easily deceived.

She was no longer that insecure, lonely girl. She had rewarding work that paid a living wage, she'd made friends who valued her, and she'd found genuine love. The uncertain, timid girl who had been hoodwinked by a scoundrel had become a confident, brave woman who would soon marry an honest, hard-working, handsome man. In New Canaan, she'd tried to hide her embarrassment and inadequacy, but in Brightfield, she simply breathed and lived her life. Love and acceptance had changed Greta, a transformation she never took for granted.

Just as she finished organizing the patients' charts for the following morning, Greta heard the front door of the clinic open and close. Clinic hours were over, and Dr. Connor had left to call on patients in their homes. She hoped the caller didn't have an emergency that needed immediate attention.

She stepped out of Dr. Connor's office and gasped loudly. "Papa?"

Her father turned and smiled. "Looks like my plan to surprise you was successful."

He wore his only suit and carried his derby in his hand. She advanced on shaky legs. "Is something wrong? Is Momma all right?"

"Everything's fine," he assured her. "Your mother is fine, the store is fine….I just wanted to see you. Is that all right?"

"Of course, it is." She embraced her father. Despite his words to the contrary, there had to be some reason he'd made the trip. "Did you come on the train?"

Her father removed his hat. "Sure did. It's a much easier trip than I thought. I walked here from the station. What a pretty little town this is."

"I think so too. Dr. Connor and his wife live in the back of the clinic, but they're not here. Otherwise, I'd introduce you."

"Maybe next time," he said with a shrug. "I imagine they'll be at your wedding."

"I'm sure they will. Have you had lunch, Papa?"

"Had a sandwich at the station."

Greta looked at the clock hanging near the door. "I'm due at George's warehouse. Would you like to walk over there with me? Or I can miss it today if you have another idea."

Her father walked to the window and looked out. "I'd planned to take the evening train back to New Canaan. That gives me about six hours to spend with you."

It was so unlike her father to leave the grocery store. Whatever was on his mind must be important. He would tell her in his own good time. "Let's walk to the warehouse. I'll show you around Brightfield on the way." Greta put on her hat, grabbed her purse, and escorted her father outside. "Who's watching the store?" she asked as she used her key to lock the front door.

"Your mother and that clerk I hired. Wesley Dawson is quite a go-getter. I might make him a part-time manager."

Greta led him down the sidewalk toward Main Street. "That's my second surprise of the day. I didn't think you'd ever loosen the reins."

Her father smiled like a child who'd accidentally revealed a secret. "Well, I've been thinking about expanding the business. Look over there." He pointed to a storefront nestled between the stationery store and the hardware store.

"Nolden's Grocers? What about it?"

"Did you notice the sign in the window?"

Greta scanned the storefront and fixed her gaze on the small placard near the entrance. "Oh. I didn't know the business was for sale."

Her father's face glimmered with excitement. "My idea is to buy existing stores and rename them. I could keep the same suppliers and contact the local farmers about produce. I'd manage the new store until I found someone to take over for me."

Greta's jaw slackened. "When did you get this idea?"

He thrust his hands into his trouser pockets and rocked back on his heels. "Actually, I've been hoping to do it for several years. I've been scouting groceries in other towns. Some of them are dirty or disorganized. It wouldn't take much to turn those places into money-makers."

If her father bought Nolden's Grocers, her parents would be living close by. "I'd love to have you and Momma in Brightfield."

Greta's father looked at the ground and shook his head. "I can't promise your mother would move here. She says she's happy in New Canaan."

Was this why her father had come to Brightfield? "You'd leave Momma?"

He placed his hands on her arms to calm her. "Nothing so drastic. Your mother and I have been married for nearly thirty years. Marriages change after that length of time. At the beginning, it was about creating and sustaining our family, but now that you're grown and gone, I have different dreams. Your mother knows I will always support her, but she got quite upset when I mentioned leaving New Canaan. I no longer have to sacrifice my goals for the family's well-being. I finally have time to do what I want."

Greta let the information sink in as she resumed walking. Her father might be in Brightfield, but her mother would stay in New Canaan. She didn't like the idea, but it wasn't her place to advise her parents. "I can't say I truly understand. Maybe after I've been married thirty years."

Her father chuckled softly. "Have you set a date yet?"

"I wrote to you and Momma that our wedding will be the last Saturday in May. I suppose the letter hadn't reached you before you left."

Her father's smile revealed his approval. "Last Saturday in May. I'll be there. Wouldn't want to miss the chance to walk my daughter down the aisle."

Relief and happiness surged through Greta's heart. "So, you approve of my choice this time?"

Her father tilted his head from one side to the other as though weighing the idea on a mental scale. "I've only met George once, so I can't claim to really know him. I did know Emile. He had a salesman craftiness oozing out of his pores. He didn't exactly lie as much as exaggerate, and he'd occasionally ask me to pay him in cash rather than mail a check to his home office. I suspected he kept all or most of the cash for himself."

Talk about Emile opened the door to shame, and Greta lowered her gaze to the ground. "I wish you'd told me those things before I married him."

"Would it have made a difference?" There was gentleness in her father's voice. He had no interest in admonishing her.

"Probably not." Greta admitted. They had reached the corner across from the warehouse. She pointed to the large sign above the double doors. "This is it. I see George's truck, so he may be in the office " Greta stepped off the sidewalk and into the street, but her father caught her arm and pulled her back.

"Wait just a minute. I have something I want to tell you while we're alone."

Greta heard a serious note in her father's voice. "What is it, Papa?"

"Is there some place we can sit?"

She considered the warehouse office, but there was no guarantee she would be alone with her father. "The bandstand and rose garden are about a block farther. There are benches there."

Her father gave one brisk nod. "Lead the way."

A few minutes later, Greta sat beside her father on a wooden bench. The rose garden was one of her favorite places in Brightfield, but the icy talons grasping her heart made it difficult to notice anything. Her father had more to say, and it couldn't be good news.

He surveyed the shady park with its freshly painted bandstand and colorful flower beds. "This is a lovely place."

Greta's breath was shallow and labored. She fought her impulse to pepper him with questions.

Finally, her father dropped his gaze and took a deep breath. Then he raised his head and looked at her. "When George met Damir, I saw something in his eyes, and I knew he'd guessed the truth."

Greta put a hand on her stomach to calm the nerves gathering there.

"Did George say something to you?" her father asked.

Tears filled her eyes. "You don't have to say it, Papa. You're my father, and I love you."

Her father's eyebrows rose, and he smiled. "I see George jumped to the correct conclusion and that he did indeed speak to you. Did you never suspect?"

Greta blinked back her tears. "I thought I must be adopted, but when I asked Momma, she showed me my birth certificate. Your name is there."

"That's right. I'm your legal father, and I've never regretted it. You brought so much joy into our lives, Greta. You were smart and sweet. When you came home at the end of the school day, you'd put on your apron and ask what you could do in the store. I loved spending those hours with you. Your mother was in charge all the other times, but for those few hours every day, it was just the two of us."

Contentment warmed her heart as Greta recalled those days. "Working in the store made me feel quite grown up."

Her father placed a warm hand on her shoulder. "I was so proud of you. Still am. But as you grew taller and taller, ladies would come into the store, look at you, and whisper in the corner. You knew they were gossiping about you, didn't you?"

"It was obvious."

"But you didn't know why."

Greta shifted her gaze away from her father. "Sometimes I'd overhear them say 'she's so tall' or 'she's built like a barn'. I thought they were talking about my size."

"Or Damir's size," her father corrected. "He and his wife never had a daughter, but if they had, she'd probably be your twin."

He'd reached the most sensitive part of the secret. Greta forced the question out of her constricted throat. "So it's true? Damir and Momma…."

He held up a hand. "Let me explain. Your mother, Damir, and I were the best of friends when we were young. The three of us did everything together. Damir married first. His wife was a recent arrival from Croatia, and I think he married her to please his parents. But Damir's marriage crushed your mother. Until then I didn't know how much she loved him. Then I heard your mother was going away to live with an aunt. When I pressed her for the reason, she confessed she and Damir had been together, and she was expecting a baby. Damir couldn't marry her, so I volunteered."

Despite Greta's speculations, she was shocked to hear the words. "Oh, Papa. How could you….? Didn't you….?"

He smiled the same gentle smile she'd seen all her life. "I loved your mother, Greta. It was no sacrifice for me. And the first time I saw your little red face, I fell in love with you. Your mother was a good wife. She took care of us, and, eventually, our friendship returned. When Damir's wife died, I was afraid your mother would go to him.

But she chose us instead. That's the power of love, I think. I wasn't your mother's first choice, but she came to love me."

One question remained in Greta's mind. Uncle Damir had been a constant presence in her life, even though he had hurt her parents. "Didn't you hate Uncle Damir for what he'd done?"

Her father gazed into the distance, as though looking back through the decades. "I was angry for a long time, but I felt it was wrong to prohibit him from seeing you. Damir's wife was sickly and never had a baby. In a way, you were the child we all needed. But don't worry about the wedding. Damir isn't invited."

Greta couldn't restrain herself. She threw her arms around her father's neck and rested her head on his shoulder. "You deserve much better, Papa."

"Oh, Greta." He patted her back. "Life is not about what we deserve. It's about the choices we make. I chose you and your mother. Now I choose to live closer to you and to concentrate on my business."

Greta released her father and sat back. "Momma said she didn't want me to marry Emile because she was counting on me to take care of her when she was old."

Her father reached into the breast pocket of his jacket, withdrew a white handkerchief, and handed it to her. "Your mother was wrong to say such a selfish thing. Sometimes, she lets fear overtake her. She imagines terrible things and then convinces herself they are unavoidable. If that day comes, I'm confident we can count on you for help, but why worry about something that may never happen?"

Greta dried her eyes. She was inexplicably exhausted but grateful fate had given her such a father. "Thank you for telling me. It seems as though I misunderstood a lot of things."

"I should have told you long ago, but I wasn't sure you'd understand. "

Greta took her father's hand. "I'm glad you're my papa. I don't want anyone other than you to walk me down the aisle."

***

Sitting next to George in the family's pew, Greta had insects on her mind. Bees swarmed in her stomach and invisible ants crawled along her skin every time she pictured herself standing in front of the congregation. She'd dressed in one of the outfits she'd bought while shopping with Hildy and Abigail, but it was proving to be inadequate armor for the battle she had to fight.

The biggest gossip in town was sitting near the front. Lilah Morton would probably want to take notes while Greta spoke. But Abigail and Hildy and Helen would cheer her on. They had no idea she'd decided to comply with Reverend Hixson's requirement, but they'd defend her if she needed it. They were that kind of friends.

The congregation stood to sing the doxology. The service would end in a few minutes. Greta had argued with herself ever since she and George had met with their minister. Her first reaction had been anger. How dare Reverend Hixson expect her to confess everything in public? But as the days passed, the validity of his request had seeped past the anger.

Almost a year earlier, she'd stepped into the church and introduced herself as Mrs. Greta Franklin. When Helen and Abigail took her under their wings, she'd told them she was married to a traveling salesman. She hadn't lied. She hadn't misrepresented herself. But when she married George in a few weeks, people would wonder.

She could ignore their confusion. It wasn't any of their business. Except she wanted to remain on friendly terms with her neighbors. And George would probably want to do business with them. If she told everyone at the same time, she'd be in a position to control the information. But if she let the gossips make up her story, there was no telling what fantasies they would invent.

And they would talk. Greta had learned that lesson well. Hearing her father clarify the reason behind the gossip had been oddly comforting. She wanted to live her life without fearing what people would say and confronting the community this morning would be a good first step.

Reverend Hixson moved from the pulpit to the center of the altar. "If you would like to renew your commitment to the Lord, or if you are in need of prayer, I invite you to join me at the altar while we sing our closing hymn."

That was Greta's cue. The pianist played the introduction, and the congregation joined the voices. *"Just as I am without one plea, but that Thy blood was shed for me...."*

No one moved toward the altar. Just her luck this would be the day when no one answered Reverend Hixson's invitation. If she went now, she'd have to withstand everyone's curious stares for the length of the hymn. Better to wait until the last verse.

Next to her, George's soft bass voice started the second stanza. *"Just as I am and waiting not to rid my soul of one dark blot...."*

Part of Greta wanted to hide behind George. He was all strength and sturdiness. She hadn't told him of her plan for fear of backing out at the last minute, but she wanted to make him proud. He'd been sincere when he'd refuted the importance of Reverend Hixson performing the ceremony, but Greta had grudgingly admitted the minister had a point.

"Just as I am, Thy love unknown has broken every barrier down...." The final verse. She needed to go. Greta commanded her leaden feet to move. Her knees trembled as she left George's side and stepped into the center aisle.

Reverend Hixson smiled when he realized she was heading his way. He settled his arm across her shoulders and hugged her to him. "I'm glad you made this decision, Greta."

Greta searched for George. Since he stood a head taller than everyone else in the sanctuary, he should be easy to spot. Greta's heart chilled as her gaze landed on the empty spot where he'd been standing. Had he left?

As the hymn ended, she caught sight of him edging his way through the crowded sanctuary. He came to her side and took her hand. "I'm not going to let you do this alone."

She squeezed his hand, sending her love and gratitude in the gesture.

"Please be seated," Reverend Hixson announced as soon as the final words were sung.

Expectant and curious faces stared at Greta. She glanced at her minister. Was he going to introduce her? Should she just begin the speech she'd rehearsed all morning?

George took one step forward and spoke in a friendly tone. "Morning, everybody."

A low chuckle passed through the congregation, and some people returned his greeting.

"Greta and I have an announcement to make. I know some of you thought no one would ever have me, but Greta has agreed to marry me."

The crowd's reaction was mixed. Some people clapped, many smiled, and a few huddled to whisper to each other.

It was her turn. George had broken the ice, but now Greta had to answer the question on the minds of many of her neighbors. "I've been attending this church for almost a year," she began.

A man's voice from the rear of the sanctuary called to her. "Louder, please!"

Greta swallowed her nerves. She wouldn't let Emile's wrongdoing shame her. She would never give the gossips power over her again. "I said," she practically shouted, "I've been attending this church for almost a year. When I first came, I introduced myself as a married woman because I was married in Madison County to a salesman for Washburn Flour Mills in Minneapolis. After a few months, he left for a sales call and never returned."

A murmur of astonishment passed through the congregation. Some women looked sympathetic, others scornful, but Greta pressed on. "I was ashamed. I didn't want to admit my husband had abandoned me. Then, a short time ago, I discovered my husband was a bigamist."

It wasn't a murmur but an outcry of shock that answered Greta's revelation. This must be quite a scandal for the people of Brightfield. The feathers atop Lilah Morton's hat moved frantically as she turned her head to speak to the ladies near her.

Greta rubbed her forehead and waited for the hubbub to diminish. George placed his hand on her shoulder and leaned down to speak into her ear. "Need me to finish the story?"

Greta shook her head. "I'm determined to get through this."

He squeezed her shoulder. "Go get 'em, champ."

When the crowd had returned its attention to her, Greta resumed. "I spoke to a lawyer and discovered my marriage was invalid. According to the law, I was never married. I sincerely hope you'll understand I did not intend to misrepresent myself, and I also hope you'll accept my marriage to George."

"She's good enough for me!"

Greta searched for the person who had shouted his support.

George's father stood in the middle of the congregation, smiling broadly.

George's mother got to her feet beside her husband. "She's got my vote."

Dr. Connor, Abigail, Andrew, and Hildy stood as well. "We're all looking forward to Greta joining the family," Abigail announced.

The congregation laughed and clapped. Only a few of the women sat with arms crossed and bitter faces

George turned Greta toward him and embraced her. Some men shook George's hand and some women hugged Greta, congratulating them on their wedding and sympathizing with her ordeal. It was the best she could hope for, Greta realized. No matter how long she lived in Brightfield or how respectably she lived her life, some people would never approve.

She no longer cared. The people she loved mattered, but no one else did. Doubt had been blown away by confidence, and anxiety had been vanquished by composure. She had been wrong about so many things but love and acceptance had helped her uncover the truth.

CHAPTER SIXTEEN

George leaned on the trunk of an apple tree. He'd kept out of sight while the wedding guests arrived, but he had a clear view of the road and the gathering guests. Many of his workers had come, looking ill-at-ease in their Sunday suits. The married men had their wives on their arms, but the single ones gathered in groups of two or three to talk.

He recognized many people from church. Their presence expressed their understanding of Greta's predicament. They realized how a trusting person could easily be misled by a scoundrel, and they were willing to accept her as his wife.

The Brightfield Bobcats were all present and accounted for. The baseball team's first game was on the horizon, and George would have to make time for Tuesday evening practices and Saturday games. Some of his teammates had teased him about not being able to leave his wife for baseball, but the team had a championship to defend. George wouldn't let them down.

His parents stood in a circle of neighbors. His father smiled as he shook hands and talked, and his mother was embraced by one lady after another. John and his fiancée, Rosalind, sat nearby. Their wedding would be next, although George had no idea why his brother hesitated. John had always been the bossy older brother who took on farm work as though his life depended on it. John was not one to share his concerns, and George had never been one to pry, but surely there would be another wedding soon.

Abigail and Hildy flit around the orchard like bees, making last-minute adjustments to the decorations or ensuring the refreshments were ready. The two of them had used flowers and lace to transform plain white canvas tents into a bridal scene and had placed chairs among the fruit trees so all the guests would have shade. George would never understand the ways of women, but he was thankful his sister and sister-in-law had befriended Greta. She had blossomed under their care and guidance, surprising him at times with her playful banter and flirtatious touching.

George wiped his brow and then returned his handkerchief to his pocket. "Who knew it would be so hot at the end of May?"

Henry frowned. "If I'd known you'd be such a grouch, I would've never agreed to be your best man."

"What time is it now?"

"About five minutes later than the last time you asked." Henry's scowl deepened. "I've never known you to be this agitated. Not even the permit office caused you so much grief."

George's jaw ached from clenching his teeth. "Reverend Hixson is ready, all the guests are seated, but there's no bride. Abigail said Greta was ready, so where is she?"

Henry gestured to the two-story building under construction near the orchard. "Maybe she's checking on her new house. She must really love you to move into a place that's not even half-finished."

"She moved all of her things into the house, and her kitten is coming in a few days. Besides, the roof is finished. She won't get rained on."

"What about the windows? Most new wives like windows instead of gaping holes in the wall."

"On Monday. That's only two days without windows."

"I noticed she chose the biggest house. What are you going to do with all that space?"

"Greta plans to fill it with children."

Henry gave a bark of laughter. "Somehow I just can't picture you with babies. Sure you're ready?"

"If Greta wants a baby, I'm willing to do my part." A sly grin lifted George's lips, and Henry laughed. George fixed his gaze on the road and bit his bottom lip. "Maybe my best man should go and check on my bride."

Henry twisted his head and looked at the guests. "Greta's mother is in her seat. That's usually a good sign. I'm glad I don't have to sit by her. She's a bigger grouch than you."

"You've only met her once."

"Yeah, but last night's dinner was to celebrate your wedding. All she did was complain about your mother's cooking and the boarding house where she's staying."

His future mother-in-law's complaints could be an omen, but George refused to be concerned on his wedding day. "Greta's mother isn't exactly happy her daughter is marrying me."

"You don't say," Henry replied sarcastically.

George slanted his gaze at his best man. "At least her disapproval didn't change Greta's mind."

"And here I was thinking Greta had better sense." Henry removed his jacket and folded it over his arm. "Her father told me he was buying Nolden's Grocers."

"That's right. He owns one store in New Canaan and wants to expand. Sounds like a good opportunity to me."

"Yeah, and who knows? Maybe he'll need a new grocery built someday."

George pushed away from the tree, walked a few feet toward the road, and returned. "Go find out what's keeping her, will you? I'm about two minutes away from going myself."

Henry raised his chin and squinted at something in the distance. "I see a man escorting a beautiful woman in a white dress. And...they're coming this way."

George spun around and gazed toward the road. Every inch of his body relaxed when he saw Greta and her father. "Finally. Tell the minister."

Henry slipped on his jacket and signaled Reverend Hixson. Then he and George met the minister at the cloth-covered table that represented the altar.

George lowered his head to speak to Henry. "Still got the ring?"

"Ask me that one more time, and I'll make you eat it," Henry said under his breath.

Three violinists from the Greenville Community Orchestra readied their instruments and stood in a semicircle to the left of the altar. At some unseen signal, they played a lilting tune George didn't recognize.

The music, the decoration, and even the wedding guests faded from George's consciousness. He only had eyes for his bride. A wreath of flowers crowned her head and anchored the veil that floated behind her in the spring breeze. Her dress seemed plain, but as she approached, he saw the clever design that complimented her height. She'd never been more beautiful.

Happiness danced in George's soul. In a few moments, she would be his to have and to hold. Everything worthwhile was worth fighting for. Greta had overcome every barrier that kept her from him, and, in doing so, she'd revealed the great depth of her love for him.

He would cherish her, honor her, and love her for the rest of his life.

Be the first to know when Claire Sanders publishes a new book. Click to sign up for Claire's newsletter:

https://www.clairesandersbooks.com/newsletter/

To find a complete listing of other books by Claire Sanders, visit her website:

www.clairesandersbooks.com

Turn the page to read a selection from the fourth book in "The Masons of Brightfield" series, "The Enterprising Bride".

CHAPTER ONE

Red-winged blackbirds called to each other as the rising sun chased shadows from the fields. John Mason listened to the birds' rusty-hinged song and smiled to himself. The little thieves would be feasting in his wheat field soon, and although other farmers considered the birds to be pests, John didn't begrudge the pittance they took from his harvest. "We're helping the Lord feed his creatures," his mother had told him when he'd been little more than a boy. Since then, he'd considered the loss a kind of tithe. He could share his bounty with birds and field mice and still have enough to make a profit at harvest time.

From his perch atop the hay mower, John scanned the alfalfa. He should be able to cut the entire field in one day if the weather held. Wet alfalfa would grow mold and threaten the entire harvest. One day to cut, one day to dry, and one day to gather. All he needed was three straight days without rain.

A farmer's life revolved around the weather. Sometimes he prayed for rain to nourish the crops. Other days, he prayed to protect his harvest from hail or tornadoes. John loved being a farmer but hated how unpredictable it could be. No matter how hard he worked, he could lose everything due to the fickle market, or disease, or drought, or flood, or…

John shook his head as if to banish the dark thoughts. He had to do the work to do, no matter what the weather had in store. He lowered the mowing apparatus and directed his horses into the field. The pungent, earthy scent of cut alfalfa enveloped John in an invisible cloud of freshness. It was the smell of summer.

Autumn brought the scents of wood smoke and apples and spring the aromas of wildflowers and freshly turned soil. But summer brought baseball. The smell of his leather mitt always kindled his desire to play. He was the catcher for the Brightfield Bobcats, 1910 champions of Town League Baseball. The first game of the summer was scheduled for Saturday. At the end of twelve weeks, the two teams with the best records would square off to determine the championship. It had always been the Bobcats and the Green Stockings, and John's team had always placed second.

Until last year.

Already there was talk of losing the title to the Green Stockings, but John and his teammates were determined to finish in first place again this year. That would put an end to the talk of flukes and lucky breaks, and worst of all, the gibe that his sister had won the game for the Bobcats.

His sister!

John reached the end of the field and turned the team to make a return sweep. He had practice tonight, and he'd invited Rosalind to meet him there. Two things to look forward to — baseball and his fiancée. Rosalind was sweetness and loveliness and kindness all wrapped into one beautiful girl. He'd stuttered badly when he'd proposed, but she'd understood. Thank goodness she'd agreed to marry him. Someday they'd live in their own house and the farm would be his.

Neither one of his brothers had wanted to farm, and his sister, Abigail, lived in town, so, when the time came, he and Rosalind would have the land for themselves. She was a farmer's daughter, so she knew what to expect. There would be long days and hard work, but they would be together.

If only his sister would stop pushing him about the date of his wedding. Rosalind understood his need to wait. When he had enough money in the bank to tide them over in case disaster struck, he and Rosalind would sit down and decide when and where they'd get married. Another good year, or two, and he'd have enough saved to live without farm revenue. Then he'd feel secure enough to take on the added responsibilities of a wife and the children that would follow.

All he needed were two profitable years, and he'd be ready to meet her at the altar.

***

Rosalind Walker removed her gardening gloves and stretched her arms above her head. Roses of every color, zinnias, dahlias, lilies, and sunflowers filled buckets of water at her feet. The Brightfield florist had doubled his order in preparation for upcoming weddings, but Rosalind wasn't complaining. She'd just doubled her profit for the week.

If her father would give her more land, she could expand her business to the florists in nearby Greenville. But her father had made it quite clear that he had no plans to indulge her hobby by sacrificing more of his valuable acreage.

153

Rosalind's anger rose like mercury in a thermometer every time her father used that word. Hobby? Flowers were her business. Since leaving home was an impossibility and attending college was beyond her parents' imagination, she'd had no way to make her own money except to go into business for herself. The neglected remains of a greenhouse had sparked the idea, and her father had agreed to replace the broken glass panes. The rest, however, had been up to her.

She'd repaired the existing shelves, taught herself how to build new shelves, and collected every suitable pot on the farm. She'd transformed parts of a broken fence into a three-sided bin for compost and had filled the pots with rich topsoil from the farm. Then she'd used the knowledge she'd gained from helping her mother in the kitchen garden to collect flower seeds and cuttings from every gardener in Brightfield. She'd spent the first winter nursing the seedlings like a mother with a newborn until they'd been strong enough to move to the acre her father had given her.

That first spring had been a time to celebrate each bloom, to weep over plants that failed, and to learn. Bit by bit, her greenhouse collection had grown until she had enough flowers to sell at the weekly farmers' market in town. Her bouquets had caught the attention of the Brightfield florist who'd relied on a grower in a distant county to ship flowers by rail. Now, in her third year of business, she was ready for a larger greenhouse and at least another acre of land.

Rosalind hoped her future husband would support her dreams of expanding the business. The Masons had more acreage than her father's farm, although there was no greenhouse there. She hadn't spoken to John about her plans, and a wedding date hadn't been determined, but her goal was to sell her flowers to all the florists in the county. And after cornering the market in the county, she'd expand to the state, and the neighboring states, and…

She laughed to herself. Rosalind Walker, queen of the flower growers. She may as well buy a crown. Shaking her head in self-mockery, she hoisted the buckets into the wagon bed and walked toward the barn. As soon as she hitched the old mare to the wagon, she'd drive into town, deliver her flowers, and pick up her payment. Her bank account was growing as well as her flowers. When her wedding day finally came, she wouldn't be a penniless bride, totally dependent on her husband.

It was time to pin down a date for that wedding. Her business needed John's support, and although he knew she sold bouquets at the farmers' market, she'd never shared her dreams for expansion. She could use her funds to build a larger greenhouse on the Mason farm, but she needed at least two acres if she wanted to sell to all the florists in the county. It would be best if she could move her operation to the new greenhouse before winter. Being able to supply flowers while the countryside was buried in snow was the ideal position for a grower, and she intended to make the most of that opportunity.

She hitched the mare to the wagon, climbed onto the driver's bench, and turned the horse onto the dirt road that led to town. She'd see John at tonight's baseball practice. That would be a perfect time to talk to him about their wedding.